About the Author

He authored sixteen textbooks and an editor asked if he had a novel in him. This unearthed a revelation... when a scientist restricted to science-fact is released to flirt into science-fiction, interesting things start to happen. His character needed a tech; he developed a solution that modelled too well, which led to a start-up, over fifty patents, and acquisition by a Fortune 500. He would live out many parts of *The Guardian* as if a future-echo came to call, and if his mind could be read, it would be impossible to distinguish what is his principal character James and what is Nigel.

The James Moore series by Nigel Cook
The Guardian
The Collective
The Mandate

The Guardian

Nigel Cook

The Guardian

Olympia Publishers
London

www.olympiapublishers.com
OLYMPIA PAPERBACK EDITION

A CIP catalogue record for this title is
available from the British Library.

ISBN: 978-1-80439-029-0

This is a work of fiction.
Names, characters, places and incidents originate from the writer's
imagination. Any resemblance to actual persons, living or dead, is
purely coincidental.

First Published in 2023

Olympia Publishers
Tallis House
2 Tallis Street
London
EC4Y 0AB

Printed in Great Britain

Dedication

To my wife, Alonna.

Acknowledgements

Thank you, Dawn, for the hours.
And thank you, Irene, for the guidance.

Chapter 1

Shadows, dark and cold – 'It must be night.' A bright light, and polished black walls sagging and wrinkled – 'I must be asleep.' His sick stomach pulled at him nervously and his dry mouth made it impossible to swallow. Heavy headed, he pushed hard on dead arms and groaned as he rolled over onto his back to take the pressure off his aching rib cage – 'I must wake up and shut off that damned hissing noise.'

The crusted floor was buckled and broken into a mosaic of jumbled plates that dug into his back, nagging him to consciousness. Still blinking lazily, a hazy arched blackness slowly came into focus, illuminated by a circle of light on the ceiling revealing thousands of round-tipped stalagmites pointing down at him like torn toffee.

Disoriented, but suddenly convulsed with panic, he dragged himself quickly to his knees and then to his unsteady feet, shouting in a drunken slur, "What is this? ... Hello... HELLO..." The only response was a reverberating, repeating echo, that came back loud and clear. He was in some sort of cave – alone.

A kerosene lamp stood beside him issuing an aggravating sibilant sound as the pressured fuel partially vaporized when it passed through the heated coil. Turning sharply, he stumbled, dropped to one knee, and rubbed his eyes for more clarity – but there was nothing that made sense. At the outer reaches of the sphere of light he could see a curved tunnel, ribbed and rumpled like gloss black draperies – 'Where am I?'

Shivering uncontrollably, he shook his head, trying to cast off the remaining light-headedness, swallowed, and struggled to ground his mind in hopes he could somehow fathom this madness – 'Concentrate… concentrate.'

The air hung heavy, humid, and stale. Dragging himself to his feet he reached for the lantern but his motion was restricted. Something clung clammily to his body constricting his movements – 'A wet suit? … Why am I wearing a wet suit?'

Lifting the lamp to shoulder height, he held it out before ambling forward clumsily – 'This is… this is some sort of… volcanic tunnel.'

Some points of the bowed floor were smooth like ripples of black satin, while others had a hackled surface as if coal had been fused into the lining – 'But how the hell did I get here?'

The path ahead was blocked by a large mound of collapsed rubble. "DAMN and blast!" he shouted.

Retracing his previous path, he mumbled, "This makes no sense. I was here for two days… had dinner at the hotel… went to my room, and then… what happened then?"

The continuing conduit all at once dipped down at a steeper grade and ended at a pulsing pool of inky liquid. At first glance it looked like oil, but the light revealed it to be water, rising and falling in rhythm with the ocean. Kneeling down, he scooped up handfuls of water, splashed his face, and stared deep into the aqueduct contemplating his options. "Well, if I swam in… I can swim out."

It was then the light exposed a small orange buoy bobbing at the far end of the pool. Grabbing and pulling it out excitedly, it brought with it an attached small white chest. Fumbling with the side catches there was a hiss as the air seal broke. Holding the light over the open container he removed two bottles of water, a six-pack of nutritional food-drink cans, three scuba belt-buckle weights, and a letter in a water-proof bag that had his name printed on the envelope.

Ripping it open, he leaned the note towards the lamp, and read.

Dear Mr. Moore,

Before you attempt what I am sure you are contemplating, be aware the sea-access underwater section of this lava tube is approximately two hundred-yards in length.

The French have a name for it – an "oubliette" – a place to forget. The perfect holding-cell. No gates, no bars, no hope...

Chapter 2

One Month Earlier…

James allowed his thoughts to wander as he drove the same familiar commute. It was a dangerous practice since he would often arrive with only a vague recollection of leaving home and then arriving at work. Traffic was neither slow nor fast, and maybe it was this unchanging consistency that caused his mind to drift. It was in this daze he became conscious of the surrounding terrain and all at once had this strange sense of being out of his natural element. Although he had lived in San Diego for ten years, he was originally from Southern England and Southern California is quite different. This quandary would probably always plague him, warping his mind back and forward about some equidistant point in the Atlantic. California was like an affluent foster parent that had given him success and a lifestyle beyond compare – and so any criticism always left him feeling a little ungrateful. In contrast, England was like a maternal parent that had nurtured him from birth and through the formative years of his youth creating a strong bond – but its limited opportunity had ultimately driven him away.

He was dragged out of this daydream when he realized, once again, he was pulling into the campus parking lot. After maneuvering carefully into a space, he parked, scooped up an armful of books, folders and his briefcase, locked the car and strode determinedly towards the University's main entrance.

James Moore was a thirty-four-year-old Professor whose discipline of expertise was electronic engineering. Being around six-foot tall, blond and athletically built, he could easily have passed for a California native.

As he approached the security guard's hut, a tall pear-shaped man in uniform glanced up and immediately rose from his chair. Putting down his magazine he opened the half-door and ambled towards James, grinning jovially. "Morning, Professor Moore... Did you have a good weekend?" he chuckled as he spoke even though nothing humorous had been said.

"Good morning, Lou. Yes, I did thanks. How're things with you?"

"Not so bad. I'm enjoying your class... you don't mind if I sit in now and again?"

"Not at all, you know you're always welcome."

Having an innate fascination for technology, Lou attended James' lectures whenever he had the time. With slight hesitation, he asked, "You mentioned the other day you have a new textbook out."

"Yes. In fact... I have a copy for you here." James juggled the pile of books in his arms and slipped out a volume.

This offering triggered several more embarrassed laughs interspersed with numerous appreciative gestures. "Well, well, look at this... this is very good of you. Thank you very much, Professor Moore."

James had on several occasions insisted Lou call him by his first name, but this request caused much discomfiture and had never been adopted. Lou was in his early sixties and his perpetual good humor gave his rugged tanned face a boyish quality that instantly warmed one to him. His thick, neatly cut gray hair sprang back from his forehead in a deep wave, and James had only ever seen him dressed in his dark blue uniform, that had most definitely seen better days.

"Well, I hope you enjoy it – better be off or I'll be late… see you later." With a parting wave James hurried off leaving Lou deeply engrossed in the contents of the book.

Packed full of meandering students, James weaved his way through the corridor towards his office. Entering through a door marked 'Computer-Electronics Engineering Department' there is a relaxed, but efficient activity and murmur from several of the departments administration personnel busy at computers, talking to one another, and in a few distant offices students talked with counselors.

James' colleague and friend, Paul Barnes waved to him. "Hurry, James, he's here. I put him in your office."

James dumped his books on a nearby desk, brushed down his jacket with his hands and ran his fingers through his hair. "Oh really… What's he like?"

"Umm…"

"That bad, eh?"

"It's probably just me."

Paul had been teaching at the university for fifteen years. Ten years older than James, he was a man of average height and build with untidy sandy hair. He had a slightly unkempt appearance and a calm and pleasant demeanor that belied his quick wit and shrewd mind. He had been happily married to Sheryl for twelve years and they had a ten-year-old son called Scott.

"What didn't you like about him?"

"Now remember, this publicity could help us secure more funding… so show restraint."

Raising an eyebrow questioningly, James followed Paul into the room. A tall heavy-set man with his back to them, stood with his legs astride studying a wall chart. His hands were thrust deep into his pockets and he rocked gently on the balls of his feet. At the sound of them entering he spun round, and James could tell immediately why Paul's first impression of the man was not complimentary. From his well-groomed head to his polished loafers he exuded self-importance and unwarranted arrogance. He glanced at them with something resembling a sneer.

Paul made the introductions with enthusiasm, "James, this is Peter Menzig of science monthly... Mr. Menzig, James Moore."

James extended his hand, "Pleased to meet you, Mr. Menzig, won't you have a seat."

With a weak hand shake, phony smile, and minimal enthusiasm, he drawled, "I'll be asking you a few questions and then I'm going to need a few shots of the lab."

"Great!" said Paul with unnecessary exuberance.

Placing a tape recorder on the desk, Menzig took out a pad and pen and with a patient tone. "Okay gentlemen, I'm going to ask you both to use... plain... simple... English... for my readers – and let's keep this... brief... shall we, I only have a limited time I can give you."

Knowing full well that if he replied he would more than likely say the wrong thing, James simply nodded. "Driving a car is easy for us, but difficult for computers. The processing speed of silicon chips increases incrementally, but we're a long way off. In contrast, the human retina, and the neurons it's linked to, can process images about a million times faster than our fastest present-day computers. So, to get smarter systems, a new breed of computer is needed that combines living neurons and silicon circuits.

"Fantasy!" Menzig exclaimed.

"Reality... I have a short video I'd like to show you."

James turned the screen of his desktop to face Menzig and the video began with title and credits and then cut to a bleach-white lab where he could see several technicians working in clean-room coveralls from head-to-toe. The camera then moved to a viewing eyepiece, and a new angle showed a microscopic view of brain cells in a jelly-like nucleus with a spider-like metallic clamp being moved slowly into the frame.

James continued, "This may sound like science fiction but it's science fact. Four years ago, we connected a lobster's brain cell to an electronic circuit made with about ten-dollars of widely available off-the-shelf components, and we were able to get this living circuit, or bio-circuit, to function smoothly as a single unit. We now have the neurons from a leech connected to a PC and are able to have it perform simple math problems."

The video now showed the spider-like metallic clamp locking gently onto the jelly nucleus. The next scene pulled back to show the dynamic clamp connected through a wire to a microchip, then pulled back further to show a microchip in a signal processor circuit, and then pulled back further again to show this circuit in a computer system.

Menzig showed signs of reluctant interest. "But how do they work things out?"

"The architecturally rigid PCs of today need programmers to define every possible eventuality. Neuro-computers will act more like neurons, breaking and building new connections until they find solutions to complicated problems using their own unique, extremely high-speed, non-linear thinking method."

"But, you can't connect organic and inorganic systems?"

"You couldn't, until we developed a dynamic clamp – it allows us to intercept signals from one neuron and inject them into another."

"Are the signals compatible?"

"A signal processor converts the analog brain waves used by neurons to the digital zeros and ones of computers."

Menzig had stopped taking notes and sat in silence. For a moment it looked as though he was about to let down his haughty facade and show genuine interest. "Mmm, so—" he stopped abruptly. "I'm afraid I'm out of time..." This was declared without looking at his watch, "...So we'll have to continue at another time."

"You haven't seen the lab?""

"It is really something to see this in action," Paul added.

"I'll send my assistant over when I can spare her to wrap this up."

Disappointed at the premature termination, James leaned back and fixed Menzig with a cold stare. Sensing the mounting tension Paul leapt to his feet eager to usher Menzig out of the room.

Before they could leave James called out, "By the way, Mr. Menzig, have you ever seen the brain cell of a swamp-loving, blood-sucking parasite?"

Menzig paused, puzzled, his bulk framed in the doorway. "A leech?"

"No... a reporter – it's quite small you know!"

With a burst of embarrassed laughter, Paul ushered him away saying, "These English, such a sense of humor, don't you think?"

Chapter 3

A hazy sun filtered through the trees and the early-morning breeze was refreshing. At this time of year, after the heavy rains of winter, everything was green and lush with blossom and spring flowers in abundance. The long low-lying ranch house slumbered in the mild warmth, while at the end of a steep stone path in a white-fenced corral a solitary rider was putting a horse through its paces. The mare was spirited, and there had been a battle of wills ensuing for over an hour. With dark patches of sweat glistening on her heaving sides, she whinnied whenever the whip was brought down violently against her flank.

The rider was Erik Banner, the current San Diego mayor and candidate for state governor, awakened at his customary five a.m.; he had breakfasted, dealt with his correspondence, and was now enjoying a little rigorous exercise. Although this exertion had not disturbed his neatly brushed blonde-gray hair, a slight sweat had started to break out across the brow of his strong angular face. Around fifty years old, he was tall, strong and muscular, and the intense morning workout had invigorated rather than taxed him. Jerking the reins first in one direction and then in the other, and kicking his heels deep into the horse's side he repeated the instructions over and over until his commands were obeyed without objection. Finally, after riding the horse around the corral at a fast pace and stopping sporadically to test obedience, he felt satisfied.

Catching sight of his advisor, Karl List, strolling down from the house he dismounted, handed the reins to a waiting groom and strode over to where Karl had taken a seat on a wicker chair in a gazebo surrounded by a small glade of trees.

Karl's thick mat of white hair was cut short in a military style, and although his ruggedly lined face put him in his mid-sixties, from a distance his fit and trim physique gave the impression of a much younger man.

"Good morning, Karl. How are you?"

"Very well thank you. I have some details for your attention," he replied with a faint but distinct German accent. The response, although polite and courteous, held no hint of warmth.

"You know…" Erik mused, pouring himself a glass of iced water, "…There's much to be learned from horsemanship. It teaches you how to rule the living animal… and whether the weak is a horse or person, the same set of conditioning rules apply."

Karl held up a newspaper and displayed the front page. "Have you seen this?"

***

By midday the heat was intense and the slight breeze that barely stirred the treetops was insignificant. The warmth brought out the heavy sweet smell of the honeysuckle that grew in profusion on the banks surrounding the ranch, and a small lizard eager to get out the glare scurried into its damp dark undergrowth.

The sun beat down on the operative as he stood on the south-facing patio and reported to Karl, who sat listening beneath a shady umbrella. The young man's mouth dried at an alarming rate, beads of sweat glistened on his forehead and then began to trickle down his face. Running his sleeve across his forehead and pushing his sunglasses up his nose, he looked longingly at the jug of iced water on the wrought iron table in front of Karl.

"Did you understand your assignment?" interrupted Karl.

"Yes sir, but..."

"Ah good. So we're not having a communication problem."

"No sir, it's just..." The agent stopped as Karl lifted his hand.

"This is important, so let me speak plainly. In this organization you are either efficient or expendable... what are you?"

Quickly lowering his report, he fixed his attention on a point off in the distance and answered, "Efficient, sir."

"Good. You may go."

With visible relief he turned on his heels and left.

Karl closed his eyes and massaged the bridge of his nose in an effort to relieve a tension headache that had plagued him all day. The umbrella offered shade from the intense sun-rays but little in the way of relief from the heat. Leaning back and closing his eyes, his head drooped to the side and he slipped into an involuntary doze.

As his mind drifted, shadowy figures and dreamy images emerged and slowly took shape. A distant memory came vividly to life – that of when he was in his mid-teens aboard a submarine.

A younger Karl sits in the officer's mess massaging his temples and stands to attention as an officer enters and pours himself a coffee. "At ease... a graduate from Ordensburg I hear?"

"Yes, sir."

Seeing his pained expression. "You don't ever get used to it... you just get tired of caring."

For these extended journeys the boat's holds were inadequate and so the extra diesel fuel and food was stacked on

22

the decks with floorboards on top, dramatically lowering the headroom. Additional supplies were everywhere – loaded in all but one of the toilets, jammed up against the bulkheads and crammed into every conceivable space. This made the naturally claustrophobic environment even more unbearably confining. Discipline, a strong sense of duty, and determination had helped him endure the first three weeks in which he had walked permanently hunched until the deck's supplies were finally used. To his credit, he had sustained without protest, many of the hardships normally accepted by the seasoned submariner – like sharing a bunk with two seamen who had not washed for weeks, and using a toilet where the stench of overuse permeated into the living quarters. Sponge bathing with a bucket of sea water may have cleaned you, but it also left a layer of salt that dried and made you scratch so badly you realized why most aboard didn't bother. Compounding all these problems was the sweltering heat below decks, especially when submerged, that pushed the thermometer well beyond its one hundred and twenty-degree limit.

These hardships he bore – but nobody, no nobody, had warned him of the "head-ache". It had to be referred to in the singular since he had been afflicted with it from the moment he came aboard and it had never left him. Initially triggered by the concentrated reek of diesel fuel; it had been maintained by the heat, the constant pressure changes at varying depths, and the lack of air quality that left your mouth tasting as though you were sucking on a coin.

Now in a deep sleep, he began to vividly relive the pain and suffering he had endured and stirred fitfully in his chair. His head had tilted to constrict his windpipe and a loud snore erupted from the base of his throat. Shocking him awake, he sprung forward in his chair and leapt up in alarm, to come face to face with two waiting operatives. One of them only just managed to remove a smirk before Karl struck him hard across the face with the back of his hand, "Something amusing you?"

Chapter 4

After finishing his morning lecture, James went into the teacher's lounge, poured himself a cup of coffee, picked up the morning newspaper, and collapsed into one of the armchairs. This dimly lit room had a mismatch of comfortable chairs sporadically set out with accompanying side tables and reading lamps. It was a safe haven for professors who had been talking all morning and now wanted a bit of peace and quiet. To encourage this unwritten law of silence they seated themselves with enough distance between one another to make conversation difficult.

If anyone had questioned James about the article he was eyeing he could not have answered – his eyes glazed and focused inwards.

"James," whispered Paul, coming from behind and snapping him out of his trance with a start.

"Ah, Paul."

"You were a million miles away," Paul said, pouring himself a coffee and sitting opposite.

"No, I was, emm…"

"What is it, James?"

"Screwed up that interview… I should have fed his ego a little – tried to work around his bloody irritating personality."

"You definitely set him back on his heels… you could have been a little more tactful. However, I think he deserved a good kick in the pants!"

"It'll be interesting to see the article… now listen, Paul."

"Aha, I knew it."

"What?"

"I'm sorry, after you."

James proceeded on oblivious. "One good thing came from the meeting this morning – I realize I've been making the link unnecessarily complicated."

Paul had been aware of James' potential right from the start and was genuinely interested in his different ideas and approaches, taking pleasure in the honest judgment and sounding board he could offer. Paul sat forward, "For the Mind-Link?"

"Yes – I think the signal conversion is redundant. Simply pick-up the analog brain waves from the sub-conscious and inject them back into the conscious."

After the successful development of the Bio-Circuit, James and Paul had concentrated their efforts on the next milestone – the Neuro-Computer. As is often the case whenever one ventures into an uncharted territory of science, new ideas seem to spawn countless spin-off possibilities. It was about a year ago when James came to Paul with the concept of the Mind-Link. His theory was to gain access to the extensive library of past memories in the subconscious mind by using their already developed dynamic clamp technology.

Paul nodded, "Mmm…so all you'll have to deal with is amplitude and phase."

"Yes… I'll give it a try this evening!"

"That means test the changes with instruments and the simulator - NOT on yourself?"

"Of course," James replied innocently.

"James, we're not neuroscientists – and even they can't explain why the neurons are doing what they're doing. We understand our hardware and software, but that's it. This could be extremely dangerous."

"I understand... honestly."

As they rose to leave, Paul clicked his finger as an afterthought occurred to him. "Oh, by the way, Sheryl has a girlfriend from work she wants you to meet."

James visibly heaved a sigh of dread, "Please, Paul, not again... Why does she keep doing this?"

"She feels you need to be saved from yourself, and quite frankly... I'm inclined to agree with her."

***

James hurried across the parking lot to his car, opened the back door and unceremoniously dumped his things in. The afternoon was hot and muggy and so after starting the engine he turned the air conditioning on full blast. He sighed with relief as the full force of the cold air hit him in the face, and reversing out of his space he headed towards the exit of the campus. Lou, who was still in his security hut, jumped up as he passed and waved vigorously pointing at his book and laughing happily.

James was eager to implement the changes to the Mind-Link so he had left work earlier than usual. There was hardly any commuter traffic and the leisurely drive gave him time to relax and gather his thoughts. It was about a thirty-minute journey from the university to the suburbs of East County where he lived. In contrast to San Diego's white sandy beaches, this area had a small community of storybook homes surrounded by rolling hills, small farms, and a golf course. The streets were tree lined and all the homes had manicured lawns and an abundance of spring flowers. His house, which was in the Early American style, was situated at the end of a cul-de-sac. It was half brick, half gray-blue panels, with bay lattice windows, and framed by trees and green lawns. In typical bachelor style, the interior was decorated with neutral colors and sparsely furnished with traditional antique furniture.

James had never been married, although he had come close a couple of times. But, believing all things fall into place at the right time he was content to let time solve this particular problem. Paul's matchmaking wife Sheryl, however, was not of this mind set and was constantly fixing him up with a variety of vetted and approved possibilities. This interference didn't bother him since it was done with the best intentions as she was a kindly soul who couldn't resist helping anyone whom she felt needed to be taken under her wing.

Pulling into his circular driveway he parked in front of the gabled entrance, left everything in the car, and hastened to the front door. In one of his earlier experiments, he had installed a custom home automation system, and as he entered his house he was immediately welcomed by a human sounding voice. "Voice verification required."

"Butler, it's me," he answered, tossing his keys onto a side table and hanging his jacket on a hall-tree hook.

Recognizing his voice signature the system disarmed security, turned on a few lights in darkened areas, adjusted the thermostat to bring the temperature to a comfortable setting, and replied, "Welcome home, sir, you have no messages. How can I help you?"

"Butler, I'll be in the lab."

The system responded by switching the rest of the house to a low-lighting level, except for his office. A door led from this room into a third garage he had converted into a lab. Although dimly lit, light emanated from an array of computer monitors and racks of scientific instruments stacked up against the walls. Test instruments, tools, and an assortment of components and apparatus lay on a large wooden table supported by a steel frame. In most regards the room looked clinical, except for the far corner, that had two leather reclining chairs on a hexagonal rug either side of a brick gas-log fireplace. This small relaxation area was like an island in a sea of technology, and it was where he often studied, read, ate and slept.

"Butler, coffee and music," he said, pulling up a padded stool and seating himself at the work-station. In response, a self-loading coffee percolator to the right of the fireplace activated, and classical music filled the room.

Turning on a modified computer he waited impatiently as it performed its start-up routine. When complete, he moved the cursor across the screen using the track pad, opened the Signal Processor control file, and made the modifications. This took some time, but after finishing, he set the amplitude to medium, phase to zero degrees, and ran a simulation. A short time later, the computer completed the analysis and delivered negative results. James had always disagreed with putting too much store in simulators as they were programmed with currently known parameters and he was bordering on the unknown.

Frustrated, he stood up and stretched his back, pushed both hands through his hair, and walked over to pour himself another cup of coffee. Pacing the room, he paused every now and again to re-examine the simulation results expecting it could somehow answer his fundamental question… would it be safe?

"Ah, to hell with it!" he shouted in defiance, sat down, and grabbed an unusual headset that had a thick one-inch headband with thin metal strips crisscrossing across the top. On the tracks within these strips was a dynamic retrieving clamp that picked up memories from his sub-conscious, and a dynamic injecting clamp that inserted these memories back into his conscious.

Placing the apparatus on his head so it was just above his eyebrows and ran directly back above his ears, he used the laptop's track-pad to activate the "PREPARE FOR ACCESS" label. The snug fit of the headset created a pressure across the ears making him acutely aware of his pulse, and he flinched as the motors within the headset turned on and the two probes moved up and down the strips scanning for their correct position. When the whirr of the motors stopped, the computer screen responded with the message, "PROBES IN POSITION, MAKING CONTACT". Following this message, worm gears activated and the clamps moved down until they pressed firmly against his scalp.

In the event of problems, he decided to set the computer's timer so the Mind-Link would deactivate after twenty seconds. James took in a slow deep breath, held it, and then let it out even more slowly.

Paul's words of warning came to mind but he quickly shut them out, hesitated for only a moment, and then clenching his jaw to steel himself, clicked START. For what seemed like an eternity nothing happened, and then his view of the lab blinked on and off, and collapsed to nothing.

Chapter 5

Sitting in the nondescript sedan, the two men watched from across the street as the children happily vacated the elementary school in the early afternoon. Both were dressed in casual attire, had short crew cuts and still wore sunglasses even though the car windows were heavily tinted. A short wiry man sitting in the passenger seat calmly looked between the school and the screen of a net-book, occasionally making entries using the miniature keypad.

His overweight companion fidgeted in the driver's seat restlessly drumming his fingers on the steering wheel. If he had whistled or hummed it may, perhaps, have been tolerable – but instead he decided to hiss out his unrecognizable tune unaware of his partner's mounting irritation.

Enough was enough, and starting at a low volume and increasing logarithmically the silent partner exploded. "Brian, will... you... shut... the... fuck... up!"

Stunned by this outburst, Brian looked away, then replied indignantly, "There's was no need to shout – I was just trying to pass the time."

"Well pass the time quietly - I'm trying to do this," he said softening his tone and pointing a finger at the PC.

An uncomfortable silence pervaded until Brian leaned over to look at the display and ask in a whisper, "Have they finished?"

"Almost, ten minutes maybe... Do you know how much an E3 makes?"

"No, how much?"

"Almost twice what you and I get."

"No way!"

"Yep… this is why I gotta get out of surveillance and into electronics."

"But you don't know anything about it, do you?"

"Are you kidding – when I was a kid I was always taking my toys apart to see how they worked. I wired up the speakers in my truck… I've always been…" Bob searched his mind for the right word. "…Electronical," he finished proudly.

"Yeah, but… teams have to stay together."

"That's right, which is why you should be studying me more and frigging whistling less."

Taking this advice to heart Brian straightened himself and with renewed enthusiasm asked, "Where is she?"

"Talking to Ms. Tits – she and her husband are boringly predictable… Ah, the e-team have finished wiring the home and are out… it only took a week to figure out their routine."

Brian pondered this observation, "Yeah… but we're all predictable"

"I'm not."

"You go to work every day."

Bob answered by shaking his head and lifting his hands upwards to imply stupidity.

"Well, that's a pattern."

"Everybody goes to work you dick head."

"And then you go home… and don't you always go to Dooley's every Friday night?"

Bob froze as he tried desperately to formulate a counter rationale, failed and so opted for, "FUCK me!"

Brian turned away, and Bob continued, "We screw up because of you and they'll blame me 'cause I'm the team

32

leader… the other s-teams are still riding me about the droid surveillance, and I'm sick of their…"

"Who?"

"Jed and Turner… assholes. So, focus, Brian, 'cause it's my ass on the line, and I'm sick of them giving me the finger."

Brian tried to contain a fit of laughter but it erupted as Bob stared at him in disbelief. "What the hell's so funny?"

Wiping streaming eyes and still chuckling, Brian repeated, "It's my ass on the line and I'm sick of them giving me the finger."

***

Having prepared himself for almost anything, James was not by any stretch of the imagination, prepared for nothing. After activating the Mind-Link, the view he had of his lab collapsed as though elastic and all was black. Disturbed by this nothingness he began to imagine he could feel the electromagnetic wavelengths gently thrumming his brain's lobes. He knew this was ridiculous since the injecting field intensity was less than that of a hair dryer. However, it felt as if he had been adrift in this emptiness for too long, and began to worry whether his vision would ever return.

It was as he recalled Paul's earlier warning that he experienced a sensation of being sucked backwards at an alarming speed through a corridor filled with revolving motion-blurred freeze-frames. This view abruptly halted in front of what looked like a large lenticular screen showing an indecipherable image that had depth and motion. His inner eye moved across the surface that appeared close enough to touch, and at the same time he became aware of a series of interlaced images beneath. The surrounding sounds were garbled and scrambled almost beyond recognition, but somehow an underlying tone was familiar – it

33

was Paul!

As he began to get accustomed to this surreal environment he was once again warped backwards like a dust particle being inhaled through a tube – an experience that was both exhilarating and terrifying. This journey lasted longer before his motion was arrested in sight of another large elliptically shaped unintelligible image. He was only afforded a split second to study this muddled vision before being catapulted forward through the tunnel of transparent images and back into blackness. Then, with an expanding snap, the view of his lab came into focus – he was back, staring at a message on the display that read, "Access Complete."

Reaching for the table to steady himself, he took in several deep breaths – stunned by the experience. This state of shock was closely followed by an overwhelming euphoria that swelled within him culminating in a loud gratifying sigh. A slight dizziness and strong sensation of heaviness consumed him as though he had just been reinserted back into his body. This was a little disconcerting at first but passed as soon as he became more aware of his familiar surroundings.

"Butler, phone Paul." Tapping on the desk eagerly, he listened as the phone rang a few times before Paul answered. Unable to control his elation, he blurted out, "Paul! You won't believe it, it's incredible, the—"

"…I'm sorry James, hold on…" James could hear Sheryl mumbling in the background and then Paul answered her, "It's James." There was another pause as Sheryl spoke again and then Paul returned to James, "Sheryl can't believe you've remembered."

"Remembered what?"

"You were right, he didn't remember."

"Oh dinner you mean… of course I remembered. I was calling to see what you'd like me to bring?"

"You lie a little too well."

James could hear the amusement. "When do you want me...
now?"

"Of course. By the way, what were you saying?"

"It'll keep till I see you."

***

Before the doorbell had finished its ring, James could hear Paul
and Sheryl's son Scott shout at the top of his voice, "Someone at
the door!"

Paul greeted James and ushered him through a central
hallway, living room and then glass sliding doors to the backyard
beyond. The barbecue billowed smoke and the smell of
charbroiled chicken sharpened James' appetite.

Paul's ten-year-old son Scott was in the steaming-bubbling
spa playing with toys and on seeing James launched a broadside
of water in his direction. James sidestepped out of range to miss
the barrage.

Paul checked him with a wag of his finger, "Sorry James...
kids!"

"It's fine, he's having fun."

Scott climbed out of the spa and wrapped a towel around
himself. He was small for his age with mischievous blue eyes and
a thatch of white-blond hair. Turning to James he asked, "Are you
staying for dinner?"

"Yes, I am – here, I brought you this!" James said, flipping
a coin into the air for Scott to catch.

"Wow, thanks... What's this one?"

"A 1961 Sixpence – that was my pocket money for a week."

"Pocket money?"

"Allowance," Paul said providing the translation.

"How much is it worth?"

"About ten cents."

"Wow, bummer!"

At that moment Sheryl appeared bearing a glass of wine, "James! This is for you." Her voice was warm with genuine pleasure and she flung an arm round him and kissed him on his cheek. She was a small woman with coarse fair hair tied up haphazardly with tendrils escaping down her neck. Her round face was pale and freckled with soft gentle features that could not exactly be described as pretty, but somehow contrived to look precisely as they should. Dressed in casual baggy clothes that had been relegated for home use only, her presence brought with it an immediate sense of warmth and welcome.

"What have you been up to?" Sheryl asked, her feminine intuition alerted by James' look of exuberance.

Unable to contain himself any further, he blurted out, "It works, Sheryl! Well, it didn't completely work, but a phase change will clear up the audio and video... It works!"

Sheryl turned to Paul for an explanation of this unintelligible babble. Paul shook his head in disapproval. "You promised."

"I'm fine Paul – it was how I imagined an out-of-body experience to be... no that's not quite right, it felt more like a waking sleep."

Sheryl whispered to Paul, "Has he been out in the sun too long?"

Paul sighed, "You know what they say – mad dogs and Englishmen."

Chapter 6

The lava tubes' wall lining was covered with time-frozen ripples but in some places this facing had ruptured before cooling and peeled back to form outcroppings, one of which had fashioned itself into the shape of a perfect seat. After testing its strength, he sat, and rubbing his empty hand across his face, blinked and squinted to help bring the words back into focus.

Dear Mr. Moore,

Before you attempt what I am sure you are contemplating, be aware the sea-access underwater section of this lava tube is approximately two hundred-yards in length.

The French have a name for it – an "oubliette" - a place to forget. The perfect holding cell. No gates, no bars, no hope.

You will I'm sure be missed. However, after a long and fruitless search it will appear as though you have literally vanished off the face of the earth. Your life is now in our hands and as a gesture of good faith we will soon be inserting another buoy and chest into the sea aperture. It will work its way up to your position naturally in a few hours.

The point, I hear you ask – we want to know what you know and how you came to know it. You will have the opportunity to answer these questions when we send in a communicator in due course.

Goodbye for now.

James lowered the note and let it drop into the chest – 'I don't understand.' He forced his mind to sharply focus. In the past he had found this extreme concentration caused such a heavy drain he typically only had a finite time to derive a solution. Once below a threshold he generally had no choice but to disconnect from sheer exhaustion and would need to sleep in order to regenerate. "Come on... I've got to... WHAT?"

The mental mists cleared and he stood. "Solve it. This is just a problem to be solved – engineer the bloody thing."

Grabbing a nearby rock he looked for a smooth surface to act as a scratch pad. "Right, Descartes' problem-solving process... One: Never accept anything as true unless it is clear and distinct enough to exclude all doubt from your mind." Reaching for the note he angled it to capture the light. "Approximately two hundred-yards? We'll see."

Placing the lamp at the water's edge and turning it to maximum, illuminated the water at the entrance and as he entered it appeared as if he were bathing in liquid light. The wet suit buffered most of his body from the frigid water except for his extremities and these quickly numbed and throbbed. Taking a shallow breath, he ducked his head underwater and gazed down into the depths of the ever-darkening tunnel in which photons struggled to travel even a short distance down the ominous aqueduct.

Fortunately, the sea held no fears for James. Growing up in a small fishing village he had spent more of the summer in the sea than out. In high school he had easily passed the lifeguard certificate and believed this would give him an easy source of income only to be thoroughly disillusioned when he took the job and was quickly bored to tears watching others enjoying themselves. The Royal Navy had put him through a rigorous set of 'safety of life at sea' classes and tests that had been challenging but not in any way intimidating. Swimming blind into the unknown, however, was an entirely different matter, but he had an objective, and paused for only a moment to take several deep breaths and then plunged headfirst into what looked like... oblivion.

Chapter 7

On the stage of the small auditorium, Erik Banner exuded his usual blend of charm and charisma that had won him the Mayor's office, and seemed set to win him the Governor's. The audience in this early evening town-hall meeting appeared to be hand-picked for the media to represent diverse backgrounds, ethnicities and ages.

His carefully crafted rhetoric was polished to perfection and held the capacity crowd almost spellbound. Shouting incantations one moment and then dropping his tone to a confidential whisper the next, he paced the stage like a preacher at an old-fashioned revival. The crowd cheered and stomped almost at his every word. He drew laughter with a witty quip, then admiration with a personal story of self-sacrifice and forgiveness, and then applause as he poignantly praised all who had attended.

Following this powerful and motivational preliminary, attendees questioned and commented on a variety of issues ranging from the economy, healthcare and teacher's pay to immigration and the draft. This accessible style coupled with his answers that blended tolerance with toughness, further captivated the crowd who waited afterwards in droves to shake his hand and pose for pictures.

Leaving the convention center with Karl at his side and four bodyguards moving in tight formation, Erik walked briskly towards his waiting limousine. It was now wet from a slight drizzle and a little too cold to stand in the dark misty evening, however, a middle-aged woman in a long black coat with anxious eyes and an expression lined with pain waited to try and catch him. Calling out his name and running towards him she was immediately blocked by the two leading bodyguards, and her petition would have been ignored had it not been for a reporter who ran over with her cameraman in tow. Noticing their approach, Karl mumbled a command and the impenetrable barrier of tall muscular operatives parted and Erik reached out a hand of welcome.

"Sir, please help, it's my husband, I—"

Erik interrupted in a calm sympathetic tone. "Take your time, and let me know how I can help."

"I'm a US citizen, my husband is a Mexican. He's been arrested for working, but he has to work – we have six-month-old twins, no medical insurance. How do we survive? Please help us."

Erik dropped his head and shook it in dismay. Turning to face the camera lens, he addressed the small crowd that had assembled. "This worries me... There but for the grace of God, eh?" Making direct eye contact with the woman, he added loudly, "I want you to give your contact info to my associate, and I will deal with this personally."

As Karl jotted down the information, Erik turned again to the crowd and thundered, "Isn't it about time you had someone in government working for you, rather than against you?" The crowd roared approval at this reprise and Erik paused to savor the response, before continuing on.

The woman grabbed at Erik's sleeve and pleaded, "Please, I beg you, help us."

Prying her loose as gently as appearances permitted, Erik

said quietly with firmness and slight irritation, "As I said, I intend to ma'am, now if you don't mind," and then climbed into his car.

As the crowd dispersed the woman was left alone watching the red running lights of the departing car send shimmering reflections on the wet tarmac.

***

After dinner James and Paul sat in the living room while James made the changes to the Mind Link system. This comfortable room had a large south-facing bay window that afforded a generous view of the back garden. The spring evening had rapidly cooled and a small wood fire flickered in the open fireplace. Bookcases crammed with books and magazines filled the alcoves and cells of soft lighting spilled from a variety of lamps set around the room. A comfortable sofa and chairs in a floral print were arranged around a circular coffee table that had been cleared to accommodate the Mind Link system.

"What is it?" James noticed Paul deep in thought.

"I was just trying to decide what I would like to re-visit. They're the obvious ones, of course – when I first met Sheryl, and when Scott was born... but I wonder how much I've forgotten. My childhood for instance, wouldn't that be a trip."

"Yes."

Paul glimpsed a sadness cross his friend's face. "Where would you go?"

"I'd like to see my father again."

"He died when you were a teenager?"

"Yes. I can see him so clearly sometimes, but then... time has a way of softening the loss while at the same time distancing me from the few memories I have left... Why do you think I was taken back to our conversation?"

Leaning back, Paul sipped his coffee. "You said at the beginning there was nothing, and then you remembered my warning."

"That's right."

"Well, the system is merely a link, I believe your mind still controls what you access. You thought about our conversation earlier and so were taken back to that time."

"I think you're right... I believe there's a sine-cosine relationship and so I'm setting the phase to ninety degrees."

"And I suppose there's no point in me warning you..."

"No."

As Paul watched, James positioned the headset and activated the system as before. When his present view collapsed to the empty nothingness, he concentrated his thoughts first on the here and now in order to stabilize himself at this waypoint before being hurtled backwards. There was a lot more trepidation this time as he knew what to expect. His anxiety was making it difficult to maintain concentration, and it felt as though he was hanging on by a thread above an abyss.

Marshaling whatever mettle he could, he let his mind go back to his meeting with Paul in the teacher's lounge earlier in the day. Once again, he was careening backwards through a corridor filled with revolving freeze-frames but on this occasion they were crystal clear. This clarity seemed to vastly improve the journey as he was now a lot more aware of his environment. Without hesitation his apparent motion was arrested before a large liquid-like three-dimensional image that moved slowly towards him and then lunged forward wrapping itself around him and engulfing him into the scene with a snap.

Paul was right, his thought had controlled the access point

since he was back in the lounge reliving the conversation he had earlier. 'Now this is going to take some getting used to,' he thought to himself. It felt as though he was viewing a detailed virtual reality recording, but there was much, much more than just sight and sound here. He was also privy to the other senses at that time – he could smell the aroma from the coffee and taste its flavor when he sipped at it. What was even more incredible, was that he was also afforded the emotions of that time – he could sense the frustration and irritation he had felt following the botched interview.

As if a fly on the wall he was able to let his inner eye wander, focusing on details he had not noticed at the time. He could study the actions of a colleague way off in the distance or read the article in the newspaper he had previously ignored. It was while he was doing this and marveling at this new found freedom and ability when he was pulled backwards abruptly through his memories to another time and place.

This was unsettling and it took a few moments to adjust. Where was he? He was in a dining room – why did it look so familiar? Why was he looking at another newspaper? These questions could not be answered before he was transported back to the lounge and the newspaper article about Carlos Ruiz. Off again, he was bounced back involuntarily to the dining room - this was becoming alarming. Looking at the top of this newspaper it read, "Cornwall Times, 23 July 1973." He was in Cornwall, a beautiful southwestern coastal county in England. His family had vacationed here every year when he was a youth... 'But why am I here?' He scanned the articles; nothing seemed to have any relevance or importance. There was to be a village fete on Saturday, a visitor had fallen to his death from the rugged cliffs near Mullion, a thatched cottage had burnt down in

Cadgewith.

He was zipped back and forth once again, and so he read the articles a little further. It was then he noticed the name of the visitor who had perished – it was Banner, a Hugh Banner. This revelation seemed to stop the nauseating oscillating action, but the stability was only short lived, and with a snap, he was extracted from the link and found himself staring at the computer screen that read, "Access Terminated."

He turned to Paul, who said quietly and with concern, "I shut it down, you were gibbering."

James noticed Sheryl standing motionless in front of him holding a press-pot of fresh coffee.

"What was I saying?"

"You kept saying, 'Erik Banner, Hugh Banner' over and over."

James noticed Sheryl staring at the headset and all at once felt a little self-conscious. Refreshing their cups she said, "It's a good job the two of you understand each other – because you're both a little weird."

James could feel his heart racing, and he was about to say something when Sheryl beat him to it. "Hugh Banner was Erik Banner's father. Well actually, stepfather. He's in all the magazines lately."

Chapter 8

The late-afternoon spring rain fell soft at times and then drenching, streaming down from low gray clouds. Paul sat patiently in his parked car staring through the windshield at the blurred view of James' home waiting for a break in the deluge. This present downpour seemed relentlessly consistent and so he opted to make a dash for the house. Beneath the porch, the noise from the rumbling gutters and gurgling drain pipes made it difficult to hear whether the door-bell had sounded and so he knocked loudly, calling out, "James, it's me."

When the automatic latch released and the door sprang ajar, Paul heard James call out, "I'm in here."

Entering the lab, he paused for a moment to let his pupils adjust to the low-light level and then seeing James at the far end of the room headed towards him. "Rough day?"

Rudely awakened from sleep, James pulled himself forward to the edge of the leather recliner. His clothes were heavily creased and disheveled and he had a thick stubble. He wiped the sleep from his eyes and swept both hands through his hair in an attempt to smarten his appearance. "I haven't slept well lately."

"I can see that."

"Butler, fresh coffee."

"Yes, sir."

Paul sat down in the adjacent chair and waited patiently for him to pull himself together, recognizing the all too familiar trademark of an obsession. "I thought I'd stop off on the way home and see how you're feeling."

"Feeling? I'm fine – why shouldn't I be," he replied irritably.

"You haven't replied to my messages and you told the office you were sick… It's been three days."

"Has it really? I'm sorry, I got a little caught up."

It was during these intense fixations Paul had witnessed James make extraordinary advances which was why he was so tolerant of this otherwise rude behavior. Science was like that – to be successful you had to obsess and let nothing interfere with that obsession. "Okay James, let's have it."

"What?" Rising to his feet, he poured himself a coffee. "Would you like a cup?"

"No thanks."

"I found him."

"Your father – I assumed as much. Was it all you hoped for?"

"A double-edged sword, really."

"C'mon James."

James stared past Paul in a trance. "I found something… disturbing."

"What?"

"I'd blocked it. You know the brain is incredible. Most things are stored in sequence, but this was filed differently… almost put to one side."

"You're not making sense."

"I've sorted it out. I'm taking care of it tomorrow, and then I can put it to rest."

"I'm convinced your judgment's clouded."

James turned quickly in irritation, "Bloody hell, Paul – just leave it alone?"

Paul responded with matched annoyance, "NO! You disappear for three days without any word and leave me to handle the project, arrange subs for your classes, and you don't even have the courtesy to answer my calls. I'm owed some sort of explanation and an apology."

This accurate assessment took the wind out of his sails. "You're right... I'm sorry. I've been rude, and my behavior inexcusable."

"Now c'mon, what's the problem?"

Collecting papers from a nearby bench, James sat down and after sorting them, presented the first. "I got this on Hugh Banner." The August 1, 1973 obituary read as follows:

Hugh Banner had recently retired after selling his company, Aerodynamics, for $175 million. In addition, he had been actively involved in local and state politics and was a key contributor to many local charities. He is survived by his daughter Judy Thompson, his granddaughter Helen Thompson, and his adopted son Erik Banner.

Seeing Paul's head lift he handed him a new sheet. "When I used the newspaper's search engine for Banner it came up with two hits. The one you just read, and this... which happened just two days later."

Another obituary dated August 3, 1973:

Judy Thompson, daughter of the late Hugh Banner, was found drowned in the family pool by staff at the Banner estate. Police believe it to be an accident as she had been on medication following the shock of her father's death two days earlier. Mrs. Thompson, a widower, is survived by her eight-year-old daughter Helen Thompson.

James continued, "Using the Mind Link I returned to my vacation memories in the summer of '73 and studied the newspaper passage in the Cornwall Times. They don't have an online archive and so I learned it by heart – here is the transcript."

Paul read the handwritten note. Police yesterday recovered the body of Hugh Banner from the rocks between Mullion and Polurrian cove. The body was discovered by two hikers in the late afternoon. It is believed that Hugh Banner, an American tourist from La Jolla in Southern California, was not familiar with the hazardous coast line and must have stumbled to his death around midday.

Paul shook his head in confusion, "I…"

"Do you remember how my mind cross-referenced the Erik Banner article in the present with the Hugh Banner article in the past, even though I was not consciously aware of it?"

"Yes?"

"So, I must have been sub-consciously aware of the link."

"I suppose…"

"Well, the same thing happened when I studied the picture of Hugh Banner in the Cornish newspaper. There was nothing special about the photo – it looked like they used the one from his passport. But… now listen to this. The moment I examined his face in more detail, I was tugged back and cycled through four events in which I actually saw Hugh Banner."

"What events?"

"The first time I saw him was in the hotel dining room at breakfast – he was also staying at the Polurrian Hotel! I saw him next in the village having lunch with an unknown woman. The following day, I passed him as he walked through the town to the Post Office, and then there was… on the cliffs."

"What?"

49

"I left my family in the cove to climb the cliffs..."

James' account just trailed off to nothing and Paul could see he was visibly disturbed. Leaning forward with his elbows on his knees, he stuttered, unsure of where to begin. "I'm not clear... where're you going with this."

"It must be set right," James said adamantly.

"So let me get this straight. You want to investigate something that happened... let's see, twenty-five years ago? Isn't it a bit late in the day?"

"No... I'm putting an end to it."

Paul was reluctant to ask, "And how's that?"

James passed him another sheet showing a picture of a young woman. "She will know."

"Who is she?"

"Hugh Banner's granddaughter. The magazine Sheryl gave me mentioned Erik Banner's niece, Helen Thompson, she's at the university in the final year of her psychology degree. I used the roster to check her schedule and she's taking a class called 'The brain, consciousness and perception' with Professor Wittiridge. You remember how interested he was in the Neuro-computer. I called him and offered to give a guest lecture on the theory behind the Mind Link – I didn't tell him it works. Anyway, he's thrilled. I'm expected tomorrow at two."

Paul rubbed his hands across his face, bewildered, and somewhat exhausted by James' intensity. "I don't know where... and what are you going to say to her?"

"I'm not going to just come straight out with it, if that's what you mean."

"We'll I'm glad to hear that... But I'm warning you, I think you're making a big..."

James interrupted, "Don't say it, Paul, just... please listen and try to understand. Something happened… I can't use the Mind Link because it's always on my mind, and so I'm automatically dragged back and forced to relive it… I just need to let it go. What do you think?"

Paul had determined years ago that when someone was this stressed and seeking advice, it was best to find out exactly what they wanted to do and agree with them. "Maybe you're right…" and then pointing to the Mind Link, "…But stay clear of that thing, and for Chris' sake get some sleep before tomorrow. If you insist on doing this at least have all your faculties about you."

Chapter 9

James ignored the meandering path that led inefficiently to the university's southern entrance and instead strode directly across the large sloping lawn littered with students on afternoon recess and bordered by Jacaranda trees. As was typical in this changeable season, the storm of yesterday had departed as quickly as it arrived, leaving in its wake a pleasant, warm and sunny day. Some students sat alone while others were in groups that either studied intensely for an upcoming test or were in a state of relief having finished one.

Entering the square-block building through a set of glass doors between granite risers, James made a few enquiries as to the whereabouts of Professor Wittiridge and was directed to a large lecture hall. As he descended the stairs that cut through the center of the stepped-seating in the semi-circular room, John Wittiridge looked up from a book he was reading at his desk in front of the whiteboards and called out in dismay, "Goodness James, you're here, I should have met you. Can you ever forgive me?'

"Don't give it a second thought, I'm a little early. Thanks for having me."

"No, no, no, it is I who should thank you, and you're being much too kind. I can't believe I wasn't there to meet you."

John Wittiridge had the unfortunate habit of apologizing unnecessarily. His deferential manner together with a round rosy face and watery blue eyes gave the impression of a beaten spaniel. His many nervous gestures, like stroking his neatly trimmed white beard or patting his rotund belly, aggravated most people excruciatingly and he found himself invariably on the receiving end of brusqueness – much to his sorrow and consternation.

"Honestly, it's fine. I'm early, and I found my way here without a problem."

"Yes, but you've most generously donated your time I could have at least—"

James interrupted, trying not to snap. "How many students are you expecting?

"About forty I think."

As James leaned his case against the central podium and removed his papers John stepped forward clasping his hands and bowing slightly. "I wonder if I might ask a question?"

"Of course, please do."

"No, no, no. I can see you're busy."

"It's all right, fire away."

"Do you... No, no, no, I should let my students hear everything."

"You're probably right."

"Unless you think you can answer it in time?"

Sighing, "It's difficult for me to say, John, unless you tell me the question."

"Yes, yes, yes... so do you think I should ask it?"

Gazing heavenwards and muting a silent scream, James uttered with restraint, "Could you please find me a bottle of water."

With students present John gave a long introduction ending with, "... So without further ado, I have the privilege today to introduce Professor James Moore, who contacted me yesterday to see if I would be interested in hearing about a spin-off technology, he is trying to develop called the Mind Link. This is indeed a first, as our Engineering colleagues very rarely have much in common with us in Psychology. Well, not exactly a first because we did… anyway, please give him a warm welcome."

James took the podium to applause and gave a short discourse on the operation of the Bio-Circuit and the present status on the development of the Neuro-Computer. It was, however, only when his dissertation turned to the Mind Link that the curiosity of the audience piqued resulting in a torrent of questions. James had studied the distant photograph of Hugh Banner's granddaughter but was unable to clearly identify her amongst the attendees. To overcome this difficulty, he made a point of requesting the student's name before he answered – if it was not volunteered.

"Yes," James said pointing to a young woman in the front row with her hand up.

"Professor Moore, Carol Miller, what are you expecting to happen if this Mind Link of yours works?"

It was difficult not to blurt out the truth about the miraculous operation of the Mind Link, but the scale of this monumental discovery had made him for the moment protective and secretive. "Well, Carol, I'm assuming that having access to our past in explicit detail for reevaluation will be both shocking and enlightening. It's hard to know what to expect."

So as not to seem gender biased, he signaled to a young man on the top row. "Sir, hypnotism can be used to access past memories in detail, and subjects have recalled previously unremembered license plate numbers from crime scenes. Is this where the idea came from?"

"Good parallel, Mr…?"

"Cliff Haeber, sir."

"No Cliff, the theory came from an experience I had years ago. When I left high school, I went to the Royal Navy's Officer's Training College to become an Electronics and Communications officer. One of the requirements was to be proficient at Morse code and I'd practice constantly encoding books, newspapers, and even street signs. It was when the code became a very natural second language I became aware of subliminal messages that reflected my present thoughts and emotions. If I was bored at a lecture, for instance, I would detect the code 'tedious', and if I was being pressed by a sales pitch I would receive 'too pushy'. This formed the basis for my theory that there is some involuntary connection between our conscious and sub-conscious mind."

More questions followed, with James randomly targeting the most likely female possibilities, without making it too obvious. He was beginning to lose hope and assumed she must be absent, when a female student who had been obscured by bad lighting in the corner of the room raised her hand and asked, "How far along are you in the development, Professor Moore?"

"I have been very encouraged by the results so far, Ms…?"

"Helen Thompson."

***

John Wittiridge let out a thunderous applause at the conclusion of the lecture that made the student's enthusiastic expression of approbation wane in comparison. Many hurried off while others collected into small groups drifting slowly towards the exit or making their way to the podium.

John grabbed James' hand and shook it vigorously, "Wow…

I knew it was going to be good, I had no doubts. I hope you know I never doubted it would be a success? What I meant to say was…"

The small deputation of students that had collected nearby eventually drifted away unable to overcome their teacher's monopoly. James noticed Helen Thompson leaving through the exit at the top of the stairs and so grabbed his case. "…Thanks again, John, I've got to dash."

Leaving John on the podium, now apologizing for keeping him, James bounded up the stairs two at a time and barged through the doors into the hallway. Scanning left and right he searched the sea of humanity flowing through the corridor and just caught sight of Helen as she disappeared through another door. Turning abruptly, he quickened his pace weaving his way through the crowds and following her through the exit out to the campus grounds. Now almost upon her he slowed down dramatically and dropped to his knee pretending to fasten his shoelace. He subtly watched as she stopped to sit on a bench in the shade of a Jacaranda tree, placing her pile of books beside her. Heading slowly in her direction he tried to think of some way to initiate a conversation, but the closer he got, the further away he was from having any idea. At the last moment he veered off, and then to his surprise she looked up, smiled warmly and stood up to greet him. "Professor Moore… my name is Helen Thompson. I just attended your lecture. It was very interesting."

James reached out to shake her proffered hand. "Thank you, I'm glad you enjoyed it."

"Do you have a few minutes to answer a few more questions?"

"Certainly, I would be happy to."

"I'm working on my thesis, technology's effects on society,

and can't really think of anything original to say. After listening to your lecture, I was wondering whether to change direction and focus on how technology could enhance certain brain functions such as memory recall."

"It would give you more scope."

Her smile gave away the set up, "In order to do this I would like to interview you in more detail on the Mind Link, and feature it in my thesis?"

Adding a suitable delay for mock deliberation, he replied, "I'd be happy to help. Would lunch suit you?"

"Thank you so much."

A short distance away, a scruffy man in dark glasses pushed himself away from the tree on which he had been leaning, threw down his cigarette and crushed it under his heel. He watched as James and Helen parted, then hunching his shoulders he stuffed his hands into his pocket and slowly trailed after Helen at a discrete distance.

Chapter 10

Arriving early, James took a table for two near a window looking out onto a small paved courtyard leading to the entrance. The Prince of Wales had been fashioned after an English public house, and James noticed how the Union Jack, Royal family portraits, and pewter tankards had been used to leave no doubt as to its identity. It's open oak bar offering various British ales, wooden tables with starched white tablecloths, and Kilim rugs on the hardwood flooring added well to the image - but it lacked the essential ingredient of age. In the half-empty dining room a few business patrons were finishing their lunch, some not uttering a word while others, suit-clad and vociferous, sparred for their voices to be heard.

Looking out to the parking lot, James saw Helen arrive and walk briskly to the entrance. She was wearing blue jeans and a white top, had a petite figure and blonde-brown hair. The hostess welcomed her at the door, and seeing James rise to his feet she made her way towards him.

"This is very nice. I didn't keep you waiting too long I hope Professor Moore?" They shook hands and took their seats.

"No, I only just arrived, and please call me James... if you don't mind me calling you Helen?"

"Oh yes, yes of course – thank you," Helen replied self-consciously.

A waitress arrived at the table. "Can I start you off with a drink?"

"Would you like coffee… or perhaps a glass of wine?" James said, putting an emphasis on the wine.

"That'll be nice – Chablis please."

"I'll have the same, thank you."

Helen hooked her handbag on the armrest and settled herself, "I want to thank you again for consenting to this interview… I had no idea what to do."

"Please, I'm happy to help."

James ordered a 'ploughman's' while Helen settled for a chicken salad.

As she spoke James noticed her smile reached her eyes, which he finally decided were gray with a hint of green. "I know this is a strange question, but you don't seem the engineering type?"

"I was always fascinated by technology, but engineering is a little inhuman. I think that's why I went into teaching – it seemed to make it more personal. How about you, Helen, did you always want to be a psychologist?"

She relied on her hands to express herself, had narrow wrists, long and slim fingers with unpainted nails, and an antique ruby ring on her right middle finger. "No, but psychology always fascinated me, and it seemed to help me understand more about myself." Helen smiled, a little embarrassed at how personal the conversation had become. "How long have you been here?"

"Ten years."

"And where are you from in England?"

She had such a natural manner about her that he found himself quite at ease. "A small ancient fishing village on the Devonshire coast called St. Clements."

"My grandfather was stationed in England during the Second World War. Apparently, he loved it there."

"Oh really, do you know where?"

As she leaned forward his attention was drawn to her slender toned arms, and perfectly slanted eyebrows. "No… he died in an accident in England in the seventies – I was only eight at the time."

James had finally reached the point he had tried to get to, and no longer cared. Helen was conscious of the pause, "Do you need to go?"

Leaning on the table and compensating. "Not at all. Helen… I'd like to see you again – not just to help with your project."

"I'm glad you asked – I'd like that."

***

Brian leaned on the armrest to gain a better view of the black-and-white video images streaming live on Bob's laptop display. "C'mon, C'mon," Bob muttered through gritted teeth. The video showed two children in a kitchen having breakfast while their mother bustled around them, and with the accompanying audio they could hear the children talking and the morning news from a portable television on the counter. It was hard to imagine what could be so captivating about this simple domestic scene but it commanded their full attention.

"Where is he?" Brian whispered.

"Shhh!"

The wait continued until a man entered the scene, kissed both children, walked up to the woman and leaned against the counter. Bob turned up the volume, tilted his head, and moved his ear closer to the speaker.

"How are they, honey?"

"I'm going to have to keep them both home. This cold seems

to be getting worse. How're you feeling?"

Taking a seat and massaging his forehead, "Beat. I called in to cancel my appointments."

"YES!" Bob shouted, punching the air in excitement and then twirling his forearm to a whooping noise.

Bob's elation triggered Brian into an equal state of high spirits and with both hands raised he erupted with a deafening, "YEAH!"

"Nothing better than being the bearer of good news!" Bob said, sending the results off in an e-mail.

Squinting, Brian raised a thumb and began to bite away at the nail. "They sure will be pleased."

Bob noticed the confusion on his partner's face. "You don't know what the fuck is going on, do you?"

Brian folded his arms defensively. "Sure I do, I think…"

"Okay asshole, what don't you understand?"

"Why are we pleased he came down to breakfast?"

"You don't get any of this, do you? So, what've we been doing here in Orange County for the last three weeks?"

"Surveillance assignment… on Peter Rochek."

"Right – who is he?"

"He's running for governor against Mr. Banner?"

"And what dirt did they find on him?"

"Nothing?"

"So then what happened?"

"The E-unit went back in and messed with the heater?"

"They replaced the guts of the heater with an old one that spews out carbon monoxide, and disabled the safety detector."

"What if they smell it?"

"This shit's invisible. You can't see it, smell it, or taste it. But it'll make you sick like the flu."

"Won't they guess something's up?"

"No, that's the beauty of this set up. A lot of heaters do this when they're crapping out. And who isn't sick at this time of year."

"And why do we want them sick?"

"Because butthead, the more he's a no-show the less chance he has. What is it Mr. List said? Oh yeah, discredit or disable."

Chapter 11

Helen followed the hostess through the entrance into the El Domingo courtyard, ducking her head beneath the latticed archway laden with the musky-sweet aroma of Jasmine. When she emerged followed by James it appeared as though they had stepped through a portal that had transported them deep into the interior of Mexico. The sun was setting and there was a warm glow emanating from two open fireplaces at either end of the paved patio enclosed by thick white-washed high stucco walls almost obscured by prolific purple and orange Bougainvillea. Their senses were all at once assailed by the smell of spirits and spicy culinary delights, and the discordant sound of convivial voices and Mariachis who sang out 'Quando, Quando, Quando' for a group, giving the restaurant a vacation atmosphere. The rawhide covered high-back chairs and heavy oak circular tables were capped by brightly colored umbrellas, and the moment they were seated a busboy delivered a basket of tortilla chips, a bowl of salsa, and two glasses of iced water.

A congenial waiter arrived swiftly. "Can I get you started with a couple of margaritas?"

James raised his eyebrows questioningly to Helen. "Sounds perfect, thank you."

Relaxing back into her chair, Helen looked round appreciatively. "It's lovely here, isn't it?"

"Yes, I've always liked Old Town, but I've never been to this restaurant, how did you hear about it?"

"A friend of mine, Maria. I told her we couldn't make up our minds, and she said this would be the place."

"Well, she was absolutely right."

The waiter returned with two large salt-rimmed glasses of the frozen lime-green tequila concoction, and after some discussion, Helen ordered the chicken enchilada and James the shrimp burrito.

When the waiter left, Helen raised her glass towards James. "Here's to chance meetings!"

"Yes," he responded hoping she had not noticed his discomfort.

"When were you last in England?"

"I went last year for a couple of weeks during the summer break. I try to go back every year... I seem to see more of England now than I ever did when I lived there – 'absence makes the heart grow fonder.'"

"I've always wanted to visit. I think I must be an Anglophile at heart like my grandfather. I love the history, tradition, and I'm always drawn to novels set in England. "Do you still have family there?"

"Yes. Two aunts – Aunt May and Aunt Rose – my father's sisters. They live in a beautiful thatched cottage in a small village in Devon. I went to live with them shortly after my father died in a car accident when I was thirteen."

"I'm sorry. My mother died too when I was very young... it's very difficult at that age... But what about your mother?"

"When my parents separated, I stayed in Devon with my father. My mother remarried and immigrated to Australia. We keep in touch, but we've never been close."

"That seems rather sad?"

"Actually, it was my mother who suggested I live with my

Aunts. Even when my parents were together, I would go there after school."

"What are these Aunts like?" Helen seemed fascinated.

"Aunt May is the more practical of the two. She moves at a lightning pace dealing with all the necessities, while Aunt Rose moves through life at a slow walk. She's extremely artistic, always writing and painting."

"Have they always lived together?"

"For as long as I can remember. Rose's husband was killed in the Second World War, and even though she was only married a short time, she feels it has left her with a greater understanding of men."

Helen hesitated before replying. "But didn't you feel a bit bored... I mean, a young boy living with two older women?"

James smiled, "You'd think so, wouldn't you, but surprisingly, not at all. May is such a character – and Rose is, what can I say, so very young at heart. In fact, there was never a dull moment. It's a different way of life for children in these small villages – the countryside, sea, caves and cliffs. Looking back, I feel I led a charmed existence."

James noticed a sadness cross Helen's face. "Penny for your thoughts?"

"Oh, I was just thinking. It was nothing."

"What is it?"

Helen said nothing.

"I never talked to anyone about how I felt after my father died, but now..."

"Now?"

"At first the sadness was unbearable... and now it's a part of me, and strangely enough, I think I'm stronger than I would have been."

"But its influence handicaps you emotionally, preventing you from ever getting close."

"Hm."

Stopping in mid-sip… "What is it, James?"

Sweeping a hand through his hair nervously. "The Mind Link actually works, better than I imagined it would. But…"

"That's wonderful! When did this happen?"

"Only recently, but that's not all, and I'm sure you will know more about repressed memories than I do."

Confused, "Children will sometimes suppress traumatic events – but, what is it?"

"This is going to sound wrong, but my original muddled motive vanished after we met."

A coldness entered her tone. "Please explain what you mean."

With reluctance, "The Mind Link revealed a memory. It disturbed me, and conflicted with a… It was your grandfather."

"I still don't understand?"

"It played on my mind as they all said it was an accident, but it… I then, impulsively, organized for us to meet."

"You mean, the lecture was…"

"Yes. I'm sorry, it was stupid, but… I'm no longer interested in anything else, only you."

Lifting her hand to her brow, she shook her head. "I can't believe I'm hearing this."

James' explanation only seemed to worsen the situation – at first Helen listened with a fixed stare and then could not bring herself to look him in the eye. He explained over and over, but to no avail.

The short walk to her car seemed to last an eternity and as she climbed in and the moment of departure was imminent he made one last desperate bid. "Helen, I'm sorry. I…"

Interrupting indifferently, "I'm sorry too, things were going so nicely – but I see now I was just a guinea pig in one of your experiments."

Chapter 12

Thrusting his arms forward and back, kicking his legs, and moving his body sinuously, James used all his strength to propel himself into the tunnel until the light faded and he was forced to slow his pace. Eventually losing his bearings he groped around in the darkness for the walls of the tube, only to snag his fingers on the vicious lava stalagmites that lined the tube-like rows of shark's teeth. Snatching his hand back he could feel the warm blood oozing from the cut. Squeezing his throbbing fingers and holding his position, he peered back into the depths in the direction he had come from. He could just see the glowing light and beginnings of the conduit at his point of ingress, and this frame of reference helped him estimate the channels continuing direction.

Turning and proceeding forward, he found his next stroke forward was completely countered by an opposing water movement. Floundering momentarily, he soon realized that this rhythmic back and forth motion of the water within the tube could, in fact, be used to his advantage if only he could synchronize his strokes to go with the flow. The problem was, however, that the path ahead was pitch black, shattering any immediate hopes that his captives were bluffing – 'I better go back and rethink this.'

As he turned to retreat, he felt his hand brush against a smooth slippery object just ahead in the darkness. Resisting the urge to panic, he pulled back and searched the murky depths –

'What the hell was that?' His lungs began to signal a preliminary, but not urgent desire for oxygen.

The limited light particles at this point revealed the round head and thin neck of, what looked like, a creature moving slowly towards him. It appeared most like a jellyfish at first, but then as it came closer, a lower body mass seemed to be present. Its approach was accompanied by a tapping sound as it slithered and swayed in its advance.

To make matters worse, his body now began to nag more urgently for oxygen. He felt a tightening in his chest, his muscles contracting and a thumping in his head. As the creature's silhouette became slightly clearer, his mind settled on an octopus or large squid – which didn't make him feel much better. Swimming slowly backwards to maintain his distance, the increased light level now revealed the creature's true identity – it was another buoy with an attached chest.

Relief flooded his system giving him the extra impetus he needed to swim forward, grab the connecting cord, and impel himself back to the entrance where he thrust his head through the water surface and gulped air loudly into his starving lungs.

Twelve hours had passed since James awoke to his forced incarceration, and a vague sense of numbing calm had laid claim to him. Sitting on a rock step he finished another food-drink and then carefully examined the empty can at arm's length as if some illusive answer would become all at once apparent – it didn't and so he laid it carefully alongside all the other items. The second chest had almost the same as the first, except for no further communication, and there had not been another chest since.

What was strange to him as he glanced around at the confines of his dreary dungeon, was that if the circumstances had been different he would have thoroughly enjoyed having the opportunity to study this now dormant lava canal. The time-stopped features adorning the tubes' linings described in great detail the events that had occurred just before this molten rock siphon cooled and hardened. On close inspection he had found shelves along the walls that showed how the level of lava during the course of an eruption had fluctuated, leaving benches, like ocean tidemarks. Towards the upper end the wall lining had burst open in several places and lava had squeezed out to form a variety of solid shapes, one of which resembled a human hand that appeared to be struggling to break in. Around him in the lower section, lava had oozed up through the floor to form embedded spheres, some of which had burst like boils with the splattering captured forever in permanent freeze-frame.

Following this extensive reconnoiter of the interior, James tried several more progressively deeper dives into the tube's sub-aqueous section, before finally accepting the inevitable – he was at an impasse. An impending sense of futility had drained him far faster than the physical output and so he sat trying in vain to resist, until he succumbed, eased himself off his seat, laid his head on his folded arms, and closed his eyes.

Chapter 13

James worked solidly in his lab until four a.m. and then, exhausted, collapsed into an armchair. His body may have been willing but his guilty conscience had no intention of letting him off that easily.

Leaping up in frustration, he pulled on shorts, shirt and jogging shoes, and headed out into a thick early morning misty marine layer. He had left an additional apology on Helen's voice mail and had, as he expected, had nothing in return. As each foot pounded the pavement it sent a jarring vibration through his body aggravating a tension headache which he felt was well deserved.

Leaving the streets of the suburb, he veered off onto a dirt path leading up through the canyon and away from civilization. Helen's final words repeated in his mind, trapped in what seemed like an endless echoing loop, which seemed to increase in rhythm as he picked up the pace.

As he looked down to see his feet pounding the dirt track, segments of the repressed memory returned…

He had tucked himself lower down on the ledge just below the cliff ridge, had pressed himself flat against the rock face shaking with fear, breathing rapidly, and desperately hoping he would not be discovered.

A shadow in his path revealed a hawk, high above, as it circled in its search for prey. Scrubby tumbleweeds grew in patches, and tall eucalyptus trees stood etched against the lightening sky… and then he remembered…

How the older man's bloodied and beaten face had suddenly slumped over the edge, and he could almost hear his younger self let out an involuntary cry that he instantly muted.

Then his foot caught a rock partially embedded into the ground. If he hadn't run himself ragged, he could have easily recovered, but his reflexes had been compromised and the subsequent fall was jarring. Just able to extend his hands out in front of him in time, his elbows and knees took the brunt of the impact and in a cloud of dust he came to a grinding halt. He remained on all fours, panting heavily, before yelling, "You stupid BASTARD!"

Rolling onto his back he laid prostrate still trying to catch his breath. Surprisingly, this shock to the system appeared to have served some useful purpose, for even though he felt physically battered and bruised, his mind was no longer reeling. Pulling himself up to a sitting position, he inspected his grazed and bloodied wounds, hung his head and rested his forearms on his bent knees.

It was as he stretched his head from side-to-side he saw a mountain lion perched motionless on a boulder about fifty yards ahead. The filtered sun highlighted the dark reddish-brown ridge of its back and glinted on its lighter yellow-gray flank. He was magnificent, and James felt privileged at being able to witness this impressive predator first hand. His small head hung low and his eyes maintained a fixed stare. From his position on the trail James could pick out the black stripes around his slightly open mouth, black spots above each eye, and estimated his body weight at around two hundred pounds.

This feeling of admiration, however, gave way to a basic primeval instinct deep within him that warned he was being evaluated – sized up as to whether he could be taken. Realizing that being seated with injuries was a weak position he slowly raised himself to his feet picking up a nearby fist-size rock. This activity did nothing to deter the cougar's glare.

The standoff continued as his mind raced and all he could come up with was that the big cats tend to have an intolerance to noise. Reaching into his back pocket he slowly removed his cell phone, lifted the phone so he could maintain eye contact, turned volume to maximum, randomly selected a bastardized version of Beethoven's ninth ring tone, and activated a test.

The shrill high-pitched fast-tempo tones broke the spell, and the puma turned away in what appeared an involuntary reflex, leapt effortlessly to another boulder, turned back for a split second with an expression of contempt, and dropped out of sight.

***

Parking in the picturesque town of La Jolla was always infuriating so Helen and Maria chose their usual out-of-the-way residential side street and walked into town. The route took them past the tunnel to the caves, and onto the cliffs from which they could see the bravest surfers battling the murderous waves on Windansea Beach.

"Isn't it a lovely day?" said Helen.

"Yes, I was reading that the Spanish Conquistadors said these were the most beautiful beaches which is why they named it The Jewel," replied Maria.

Maria was a short Hispanic woman of indeterminate age with round rosy cheeks and a plump matronly figure. To an outsider she would probably be described as more homely than pretty but her bright kind eyes and gentle manner immediately warmed one to her.

The sun was at last beginning to break through the off-shore flow allowing a little warmth to offset the slightly chilly breeze, and the upscale well-established Prospect Street was filled with the usual stark contrast of occupants. Young mothers jogged behind free-wheeling strollers, surfers chatted to preppy students in sidewalk cafes, and older well-groomed tourists shopped in the many boutiques and novelty stores.

Cutting down Herschel Street, Helen stopped to browse through a rack of summer T-shirts and skirts outside a small dress shop aptly named Skirts'n'Tops, while Maria went into the Marble Slab Ice Cream Parlor next door returning with a double scoop of cookies-and cream ice cream in a waffle cone.

"So, when are you goin' to tell me what is wrong."

"There's nothing wrong – I just didn't want any ice cream," she said continuing to flick irritably through the rack.

Maria casually thumbed through some of the tops, "These must be for midget girls… You may grow up to be good psychologist, but you are no' good actress… Oh, I want to pick up some oatmeal cookies from that Cheese Shop for Alberto."

"Maria, there's nothing wrong, I just have a bit of a headache."

Maria led her to a sidewalk coffee shop. "Okay, let me get you one of those latte coffees for the headache and then you can tell me what is matter."

Helen resigned herself to Maria's ministrations and sat down outside the café while Maria ordered, and then returned with coffee and a bagel with cream cheese.

"What's this?"

"Just little snack for you – you too thin." Maria almost slipped off the small chair and in irritation called out to the uncaring counter assistant. "What with this tiny chair? Do they think we are all piggies!"

Helen could not help but smile. "I think you mean pygmies, Maria."

"Whatever... now you tell me."

So, Helen told Maria about James, his ulterior motive, and how she felt betrayed and ill-used. Maria waited until she had finished and was silent for a moment, thinking.

"So, why he tell you what he had done?"

"I think he was feeling guilty."

Maria took Helen's hand in hers and said gently, "Sweetie, people only feel guilty for people they care about."

Helen pulled her hand away. "No, Maria, I won't forgive him."

Maria shook her head and tutted. "Well, okay. But you are wrong. Okay, he makes bad mistake but he tries to fix it. Some people never say they are wrong – I think he should get second chance."

"I want to, Maria, I really do, but I don't want to be..."

"Hurt? Sweetie, what is worse – to live lonely and confused as you do, or to take chance to have real happiness?"

"He left a couple of messages."

"That is good – no? Don't be so cold Helen – I see this in you, is no' good."

Smiling, Helen leaned over to kiss Maria on the cheek, "What would I do without you to bully me."

Maria patted Helen gently on the cheek. "You a good girl. Now, eat and then we go... I not get those oatmeal cookies for Alberto – he getting a little too fat!"

Chapter 14

James' Sunday morning seemed destined to go from bad to worse. He wasted over an hour looking for some papers he remembered filing in a 'safe location' that was never to be found again. He worked for an inordinate amount of time on a new manuscript only to get stuck reading, editing, and rewriting the same paragraph to end up with a result he disliked more than the original.

His editor had left three messages and a university admin. Assistant too, and he could hear the increasing level of frustration creeping into each successive unanswered inquiry. Paul had once described these blinkered bouts of his as an 'obsessive repulsive disorder' – there was no excuse, so he left voice-mail updates and apologies for both.

"Butler, any calls?"

"No, sir."

Having designed the home automation system this was a senseless question since he knew he had programmed it to notify him of messages the moment he returned home. Picking up the phone he punched out the first few digits of Helen's number, and then decided against it.

"Bugger," he mumbled.

To which the electronic butler replied. "Yes, sir. How can I help you?" On any other occasion, this voice recognition confusion would have been funny but in his present state of mind it didn't even rank as pithy.

Slumping back in his chair James felt lethargy envelop him, and when the phone rang he didn't respond immediately, but just stared blankly at the handset for a time before recognizing Helen's number. Snatching the handset from its cradle, he took a deep breath and calmly said, "Hello?"

"It's me." Helen's voice sounded neutral. "I got your message, and I've been thinking about what you said."

"Thanks for calling, Helen... I'm sorry."

"I have this phobia, you see, about people not being what they seem."

"I understand, but please give me a second chance... Are you busy today?"

"No, I was trying to work on my thesis but I gave up – couldn't concentrate."

"I was up half the night working on something and I'd like you to see... Could you come over?" The response was not immediate and so he added, "Or we could meet somewhere else if you prefer?"

"No, no – that would be nice, and I'd like to see your house."

***

"Helen, you found it okay?" said James as he walked out to greet her.

"Yes – this is a beautiful area."

"Helen..." James reached out his hand, she moved towards him, and they kissed.

As they reluctantly pulled away from each other, she said, "I've been miserable."

"Me too... would you like some tea?"

The tour ended in the lab with Helen inspecting a headset

and comparing it to another. "Why are there two?"

"That's what I was working on till late." Picking up the other headset he explained, "This is the primary headset and it has a retrieving probe to pick up memories from the sub-conscious, and an injecting probe to insert them back into the conscious. Now, the headset you're holding is a repeating headset, which means it simply repeats whatever memories are picked up by the primary headset."

"I see, so if you use the primary headset and I put on the repeating headset, I could witness whatever memories you access."

"Exactly. Now, I haven't tried this with a repeating headset, so I don't know how you feel about that?"

"I want to try, it sounds incredible. What do I have to do?"

Pulling up a chair for Helen and one for himself he turned on the notebook computer and placed the repeating headset on Helen. "You won't have to do anything. The room will appear to blink and then black out when I activate the system, and after a short passage through a timeline tunnel I'll show you England, through my eyes. Actually, my eyes when I was twelve."

Helen was speechless and showed no fear whatsoever, but then seemed anxious. "What are you going to show me?"

"I'm going to concentrate on a small village called Mullion in Cornwall. We vacationed there, often, you sure you're not nervous?"

"Absolutely not." Helen settled herself comfortably in her chair, and as James positioned the primary headset on himself and went through the initialization, she said, "Will it feel like I'm really there?"

"Yes. You'll be aware it's a playback, but you should sense everything I felt at that time – it's repeated down to the smallest detail."

Helen squeezed the armrests as the probe moved into position.

"Just relax, the initial sensation is a little weird but it doesn't last long."

"I'm not worried in the least."

Helen waited with anticipation. She had studied at school how Raleigh had set out to find a new world called Virginia; and how English rebels had sailed on the Mayflower in search of a new England. She considered England's rich history an extension of her own, and this coupled with the idea of what this system was actually doing had her heart racing with excitement.

After James had activated the Mind Link system she saw the lab black out and after the unusual transport an image enveloped her. As warned, it was slightly unnerving to begin with, but Helen was soon distracted as she marveled at the clarity and lucidity of the surrounding images. She could see a rocky path running alongside a rugged coastline, and a few white puffy clouds in an otherwise clear blue sky. It was then, a sensory awareness seemed to engage, and she could feel the sun on her face, hear the seagulls cry above her, and smell the fragrance of the heather along the hedgerows.

This memory of James' had him following a man who turned as he walked and in a strong English accent said, "Come on James, pick your feet up. There's a church in the next cove that's over eight hundred years old. Let's go and explore."

She then heard the young James reply, "Okay, Dad."

As snippets of playback continued from this fortnight vacation she saw many beautiful old places and the history she had learned came vividly to life. It was easy to imagine Caesar's legions marching down the old cobbled roads, King Arthur and his knights riding into battle down the slopes of the rolling hills, and the gardens in beautiful stately homes being trampled down by Cromwell's armies. She saw little villages that were standing during the War of the Roses, once impenetrable castles with moats that were now homes to swans and their signets, and barren blustery moors with wild ponies and larks singing high above.

When the images blacked out and the lab was again in view, she sat transfixed. "That was absolutely incredible! Better than I ever could have imagined."

James removed both headsets and deactivated the system.

"But tell me, James, you mentioned a memory of my grandfather?"

"I wanted to put all of that behind us – it's not important any more."

"It is to me... Does the memory still disturb you?"

"No... it did at the time, but not now that I'm witnessing it through adult eyes."

"Then why the reluctance?"

"It's not for my sake."

"For mine?"

"Yes."

"But my grandfather died accidentally when he fell..."

The Butler interrupted her, "Excuse me, sir, a person has approached the front door but not rung."

Looking around in astonishment, Helen asked, "Who was that?"

"An electronic butler," replied James. "It's something I put together a few years back."

"... And it talks to you?"

"Yes... Butler, are they still there?"

"Yes, sir, but the party is leaving."

"…And you talk back to it?" Helen asked incredulously.

"Yes, it will only respond to my voice pattern."

"What's it talking about?"

"Sir, they are returning."

"Someone can't seem to make up their mind. Butler, security status?"

"The living room motion detector is fluctuating, sir."

"Okay, they appear to be looking through the window. I think I should meet our guest. You stay here, Helen."

"No, I'm coming with you."

It was about six in the evening and there was still ample light. James and Helen left the house through the back door, quietly exited through a side gate to the front yard, and came up behind the man looking through the window adjacent to the front door.

As he turned and came face to face with them, he backed away in surprise, his bland expression changing to one of extreme embarrassment.

"Can we help you?" James asked obligingly.

Chapter 15

The stranger tried quickly to compose himself, and in a voice of authority announced, "Detective Peter Hammond, San Diego Police Department." To add additional authority he straightened his back, removed his wallet and with a flourish displayed his identification. Although dressed in a suit and tie he had a naturally disheveled appearance. His face had character, and though his hair was thinning he appeared to be younger than they had originally thought.

James took the identification from him studying it in detail, and coldly asked, "Is it customary to gape into a person's home without first checking to see if they're in?"

"I tried the doorbell but I guess you didn't hear."

"Oh, really. Butler, when was the front door bell last activated?"

The man looked around, flummoxed as to whom James was addressing.

"The front doorbell was last used two days ago at 6.12 p.m., sir, which was Tuesday the twenty-third of…"

"Butler, enough, thank you." James turned to face the confused and visibly embarrassed stranger.

"Now listen, your friend must be mistaken," he pointed into the house disturbed at not being able to face his accuser.

"You're lying, and unless you want to explain yourself, we'll let the real police sort this out."

Helen had been studying the man, and it suddenly dawned

on her. "I've seen you before... on several occasions now I come to think of it – who are you really?"

James called the police department using his cell phone and spoke with a sergeant who confirmed his identity. As he was about to address his complaint a plea crossed Pete's face and James ended the call, looking to Pete to reciprocate for this gesture of good faith.

With a nod of acknowledgment, Pete conceded. "I am a police officer, and my name is Pete Hammond...and I have been following Ms. Thompson, but would like an opportunity to explain?"

"I think that's a very good idea," said Helen incredulously.

James held open the front door. "Let's go through to the living room."

James and Helen exchanged a questioning look as they followed Pete through. Without invitation he threw himself into an arm chair, looked around the room approvingly, and with an intensity that had been present from the start launched into an explanation as James and Helen seated themselves on the sofa opposite.

"After my Mom died about a year ago, I moved back into the family home and started fixin' it up and discovered a file of my Dad's called 'The Hawthorne Case' in a hidden safe in the garage. He was also a homicide detective, retired in '68, and started taking odd jobs as a private investigator. The file described a case he completed in '73 for a Helga Hawthorne from Cawnwhorl, England."

"Cornwall," James added the correction.

"If you say so... She wanted my Dad to find her son who was lost during the confusion when the Allies invaded Berlin at the end of World War II."

Fixing a stare on Helen, Pete asked, "That year… 1973. Ring any bells, Miss Thompson? Mean anything to you?"

"No," she replied, puzzled.

"It means something to me," James butted in, leaning back in his seat and crossing his legs in a relaxed manner.

"Is that a fact…" said Pete glancing momentarily at James and then returning his full attention to Helen, "…Ever been to Cornwall? Or heard the name Helga Hawthorne?"

"No – should I have?"

"I've been to Cornwall, many times on vacation. In fact, I was there in '73," James injected into what appeared to be Pete's own word association game.

Sighing irritably at being interrupted again, he asked with disinterest, "Good… you enjoy it?"

"Oh yes. Very much so."

Returning to Helen, Pete continued. "Helga believed her son was in the care of a sixteen-year-old German boy who had gone to South America and entered the US through San Diego as a war refugee in 1945. Helga married a British Army sergeant who was part of the British Post-War Monitoring Force. In 1947, her husband left the army and took his wife back to his home in Cornwall, England."

"Where in Cornwall?" asked James.

"I think it's called Catchwitch."

"You'll find that's pronounced Cadgewith."

"And I suppose you've been there too?" Pete asked sarcastically.

"I have, as a matter of fact."

Not bothering to respond, Pete continued his account. "Helga couldn't find her son using the services in England and Germany so she looked for a San Diego private detective, since this is where they entered. My dad took on the case in 1970, and because of his connections in the force and immigration he was able to find the boy."

"Oh good," said Helen, now quite captivated by the story.

"Yeah, anyway, he wrapped up the case in the summer of '73, and it was soon after he noticed he was being tailed. He had a gut feeling it was something to do with the Hawthorne case so he copied the file and placed it in the home safe. Have you ever heard of my father, David Hammond?"

"No. I haven't."

"And your grandfather, Hugh Banner. Did you ever hear him mention the name Hammond or Hawthorne?"

Bewildered, but now interested in the revealed link, she leaned forward. "No, I was only a child when my grandfather died, but what has my grandfather got to do with all this?"

Pete's eyes narrowed as he attempted to determine whether she was holding anything back, but he realized she hadn't a clue as to what he was talking about. "I'm sorry, but I've gotta run. Here's my card Miss Thompson, please call me if you think of anything."

Reaching the front door ahead of them, he stepped outside, and turned. "Where's your little friend with the sad life? Hasn't he got anything better to do than make notes on when the front door bell is rung?"

"It's a home automation system."

"Okay, see ya."

"You know what's interesting?" James called out as Pete crossed the lawn.

"What's that?" Pete stopped abruptly.

"You never did explain the link between this Hawthorne case and why you've been following Helen."

"Yeah, well… maybe another day."

"Tomorrow. I'm sure you searched who I am and where I work. My class finishes at noon, I'll see you then."

Having no interest in listening any further to James' nostalgic vacation reminiscences, Pete smiled sarcastically. "Kinda busy tomorrow."

"One more thing."

Pete turned again, this time openly showing irritation and impatience.

"I met Hugh Banner in Cornwall, in the summer of '73…" James said smiling, and just before closing the door added, "… See you tomorrow."

Staring into space with a dumbfounded expression, he mumbled, "Shit – who the hell is that guy?"

Chapter 16

Karl stirred in the darkness of his room. He had shed his bedspread and opened the window wide before retiring, but the temperature had plummeted in the night bringing him uncomfortably to a semi-conscious state, and the recollection continued...

Skimming across the ocean towards an anchored fishing vessel and at about a hundred yards from that there appears to be a metal pipe coming up from below. About two miles off the New Jersey coast, it is two a.m. on November twenty-second, 1941. His mind has him traveling down through the pipe, through multiple lenses to be ejected out of the periscope and onto the Bridge of an Undersea-Boat where a tense sub-mariner crew and several blackened face commandos stand ready.

The Captain flips up the handles. "Periscope down – Blow ballast, slow." And the orders are repeated by his First officer. "Ready away party – execute mission Bauernopfer."

The U-boat quietly surfaced and the hatches on its forward deck opened, and six heavily armed men rushed out, climbed into rubber dinghies and rowed to the trawler.

In the main cabin of the fishing vessel, four fishermen played cards and didn't move a muscle as their vessel was overrun by a well-trained and heavily-armed German boarding party. Young Karl is with them and holds a gun to the head of one of the American fishermen.

"Who is the Captain?"

A wiry older fisherman wearing a stained blue-white hat raises his hand nervously. Pulling all the other men away from the table, the German commander clears the table rapidly with a swipe of his arm, pulls out a map from his inside pocket, lays it on the table, and sits opposite.

The trawler captain looks on, with fear and confusion while the German commander points to some markings on the map. "You're lost?"

"Nein. Attention." Pointing to more than two-dozen marks on the map just north of the Hawaiian Islands. "Maybe two weeks, maybe less." Placing his finger on the points and tracing it down to the island of Oahu. "Understand?"

"But why?"

The German commander stands, leaving the map. "We leave you all unharmed. Do not lift anchor for one hour. We can hear. Understand?"

"Yes."

The boarding party left as quickly as they arrived, and if it were not for the map, the crew would question whether the incident actually happened. Leaning forward, the trawler captain studied the map that is in German, and the cluster of marks identified with a Japanese flag.

The alarm rang and his eyes opened. Heaving himself onto the edge of the bed he turned on the bedside lamp and glanced at the time – 5.25. His room and adjoining bathroom in the south wing was the epitome of minimalism, and although more spacious suites were available, the proportions of this room suited him perfectly. There was very little furniture – a single bed and side table, a large armoire, a dresser with his personal effects laid out neatly on top, and a solitary wooden chair in the corner. This starkness and the lack of any pictures on the wall was the way he liked it – undemanding and practical for the sole purpose of washing, sleeping and dressing.

After a shave and shower, he dressed in a dark gray-blue vested suit, a new white shirt, and paisley tie. After running a brush through his thick mat of white hair, he checked his appearance in the mirror of the dresser. From here he lifted an antique pocket watch and chain, and after verifying its operation, attached the chain to his waistcoat and slipped the watch into the opposite pocket. His Luger handgun was then polished before being holstered and the cloth folded and returned to its position. A Parker pen and small black book were slipped into his inside jacket pocket, and finally his wallet and a Swiss army knife were slotted into his back and right trouser pockets respectively.

Leaving his room, he made his way down the long carpeted hallway to the dining room that is traditionally appointed, and there he found Erik sipping coffee and reading the LA Times in a relaxed manner. Seeing Karl enter the room, Erik lowered his paper and looked up, "Good morning, Karl."

"Good morning, Erik."

"Getting an early start?"

"Thought I would. I've got quite a full schedule today."

A generous breakfast fare was laid out on a serving table but Karl took only some wheat toast and coffee before sitting opposite.

"Not exactly a hearty breakfast, Karl… remember, an army marches on its stomach."

"I only ever eat light this early," he replied buttering his toast and spreading on a thin layer of orange marmalade.

Erik folded the paper. "I'm glad I caught you, Karl. I read

the opponent report you e-mailed yesterday – job well done."

"Yes, indeed."

"What of the bauernopfer?"

"On schedule."

"Good. As things seem to be well in hand, you should take a break – have a vacation."

"I need no time off – my work is important and the routine suits me."

"I know that, Karl, but it's for your sake I mention this. You work tirelessly, seven days a week, and well… I just thought it might be good to get away."

Karl returned a half-eaten slice of toast to the plate and pushed it to one side with slight irritation. "I neither require it, or desire it. And I do not have anyone here who could take my place… your consideration is appreciated. I have had order and discipline in my life from the age of seven when I was sent to a military boarding school. It is a pattern I am quite used to."

"So there's no place you would like to go to, or person you would like to visit?"

On reflection, Karl replied, "Years ago I returned to Germany – it was not the same."

"Changed?"

"Castrated. I should not have gone back – I would have preferred to live with the illusion."

"What about an evening out with some female companionship."

Karl was being badgered. "Why don't you come to the point, Erik?"

Erik lifted both his hands in a gesture of innocence and returned to his paper. "I would just like to see you kick back and relax every now and then."

"Why?"

Erik smiled at how much irritation could be injected into a single word. "It would make me feel a little better if I understood your reward system."

Karl nodded, finally understanding the line of questioning. "You and I are quite different, Erik, and if it will put your mind at ease to understand my 'reward system' as you call it, then I will tell you. When I was younger I made arrangements for female companionship when the need arose as it was a distraction to my work, but now, sex is only a description of gender. Your girlfriends are high on your priority list, along with thoroughbred horses, cars, and travel. This is where we differ. I judge a person based on their character and not on their material content..."

Erik interrupted indignantly, "...hang on a second, Karl. I was just saying..."

Karl continued, "...You were trying to determine my motive as that is the key to truly understanding a person. I can see why it eludes you."

Erik folded the paper and slapped it down on the table. "Enlighten me."

"Willingly. I get no satisfaction from rewarding myself with a vacation, new car, or a night on the town. These material trinkets are fickle and their dividend momentary. Real rewards cannot be obtained easily, they require hard work and dedication, but the 'reward' is infinitely more satisfying... I take pride in fulfilling my duties to the very best of my ability. I strive to be more efficient, resourceful, loyal, thorough and relentless, all the attributes I believe truly add to the value of an individual's character."

Erik smirked, "I see. Well, if you're happy, who am I to complain!"

Chapter 17

With his usual exuberance Pete swung open the door and burst into the class. Once in, however, he was frozen in his tracks by the glare of more than thirty seated students who had turned to see the sort of person who would show up this late for a lecture. Just for a moment he felt as though he was back in high school experiencing that old familiar feeling of discomfort at being tardy. A student nearby, sympathetic to his predicament, pointed to a vacant seat. Although not generally prone to clumsiness, he had a foreboding fear he may trip up on the way and so very carefully placed one foot in front of the other as he traversed to the safety of the seat.

James wrapped up the lecture, answered student questions, tucked his notes into his briefcase, and joined Pete shaking his hand warmly. "Thanks for coming. Would you like a coffee?"

"If you'd like."

They walked the length of the corridor in total silence, prompting James to inquire, "Everything all right?"

"I thought I'd let you do the talking."

Arriving at their destination they merged into the crowd milling about the entrance to the University cafeteria. Typical of its type, the restaurant was not particularly comfortable with steel tables and chairs set out randomly and an odd dusty plant placed here and there in an attempt to add some element of life to the otherwise clinical surroundings. It was packed with chattering students and the smell of fresh coffee and unappetizing food filled the air.

With coffees in hand James led Pete to a quiet table in the corner. Realizing Pete was holding fast to this 'you do the talking first', James took the initiative. "I completely understand why finding your father's case file has motivated you to investigate a possible link to his death... They didn't find the culprit I assume?"

"No, and believe me they rallied – he had many good friends in the force."

"I'm sure – and this new information has given you some leads?"

"I think so."

James was still sensing resistance. "Simple question, Pete – do you think we can work together?"

Pete studied the man before him. "I guess... but I can't for the life of me see how you fit in?"

"Well, let's just say the link was an accident, but it has given me great insight. Ultimately, you have some pieces to this puzzle, and you know I have some too, and combined, we might just be able to make some sense of all this."

"How do you want to start?"

"To feel comfortable, how about quid-pro-quo?"

"I'd prefer tit-for-tat."

***

Helen's family home was nestled in the hills of La Jolla. James pulled up in front of a set of closed security gates that had a console built into the gates right pillar and a video camera mounted high above it. Before he was out of his car Helen's voice was heard. "Hi, James, I'm running a little late. Come up to the house. I won't be long."

The security gates opened. "Take your time, Helen – there's no rush."

A high wall encircled the estate, and the driveway meandered around a small lake and led up to a magnificent early-American brick house on a hill surrounded by immaculate landscaping. The house had a covered entrance supported by four white Colonial-style pillars, and James pulled up, behind a limousine and two men talking on the lawn some distance away. On seeing James arrive, they turned and stared for a moment, and then returned to their conversation.

Leaving his car James crunched across the noisy gravel to a large ornate front door which opened before he reached it. Maria appeared in the doorway wearing a domestic uniform and looking him up and down, outwardly demonstrating instant approval. The enthusiasm of her greeting was infectious and he could not help but respond warmly.

"My name is Maria, and I 'ave been told by 'elen to take good care of you."

"How kind of you."

"Is okay, is okay."

As they approached the door, a distracted Erik hurried out and was forced to modify his course at the last moment to avoid a collision. About the same height and build as James, he was smartly dressed in a tailored suit and James recognized him immediately.

"I'm sorry… I wasn't looking where I was going."

"That's okay, no harm done," replied James.

"You're not here to see me I hope?"

"No, no, no, no, no, he's here to see Helen," explained Maria.

"Oh I see. Erik Banner, by the way."

"James Moore. A pleasure."

The two men shook hands.

"English?"

"Yes."

"I've been to England on several occasions. A beautiful country steeped in tradition and history. Anyway, nice to have met you."

"Likewise."

Climbing into the car, James and Maria watched it depart.

"What are you two doing out here?" Helen asked reaching for James and kissing him.

"You look lovely," he said, returning the kiss and admiring her from head to toe.

"I hope this place is not too dressy."

"Oh no… you look perfect."

"Thank you, James."

Maria watched this lover's exchange with delight. Realizing they were ignoring her they both began speaking at the same time, and after the second round of each offering to let the other go first, Maria decided it was time for them to go.

The restaurant was a two-minute drive, in a shopping mall that catered exclusively to the growing Indian community. There were market stores with all manner of spices, clothing outlets with Saris for all occasions, and a miniature Hindi temple. The restaurant's frontage was dramatically fashioned after the Taj Mahal to draw western clientele with four domed corners and a white marble façade, and stood out in stark contrast to the drab surrounding red sandstone buildings. The interior was dimly illuminated with carved-marble screens, Eastern music played softly, and after a hearty welcome they were escorted to their table.

"Maria's very sweet – how long has she worked for you?"

"My mother hired her and her husband, Alberto, before I was born. They live in a cottage at the southern end of the estate and have two grown sons who are both married and live in Mexico. Alberto takes care of the grounds, and Maria is our housekeeper, although she is more than that to me."

"I could tell."

Helen had been trying to decipher the menu when a waiter arrived with pad and pen in hand. "You'll have to order for me, James."

"That's okay, I know exactly what we'll have. Crisp popadoms to start, followed by Chicken Tikka Masala and Aloo Gobi with an order of garlic Nan bread, pilau rice, mango chutney and cucumber raita." After selecting a wine they both liked, the waiter left.

"It sounds exotic."

"I hope you'll like it."

"I'm sure I will – now, stop keeping me in suspense, and tell me how it went with Pete."

"At first he held back, but soon opened up. He had brought his father's case file with him."

As Helen listened, James began by telling her about the letter from Helga to Pete's father, that described how she had been working in a munitions factory about twenty miles outside Berlin, and that her sister had been taking care of her four-month-old son during the day. In late April of 1945 the factory workers were captured by an advance British Commando unit and detained for over two months. When finally released, she went immediately to her sister's home accompanied by a British army sergeant she had befriended named Colin Hawthorne.

Unfortunately, her sister had been killed during a bombing raid and the baby had been put in the care of an older German boy who had escaped on a freighter heading for Argentina. Helga married the Army Sergeant later that year and in 1947 he left the army and returned with his wife to his home in Cadgewith.

James paused in his explanation as the wine was served, and then continued to paraphrase the report. Helga had apparently tried to locate her son using the missing relative agencies in England and Germany, but to no avail. In 1970, she tracked down one of her girlfriends who had been living in Argentina since the war, and was told the older boy and her son had entered the United States through San Diego in the fall of 1945. Going through the San Diego Chamber of Commerce she found Pete's father and he took on the case in 1970.

"Pete's father completed his assignment in the summer of 1973, reported his findings to Helga, and shortly thereafter noticed he was being tailed and so he placed a copy of the file in a hidden home safe."

"What's that?" Helen asked pointing to a batch of papers James was tucking away in a folder.

"A copy of a police report Pete gave me – it describes the scene in quite graphic detail."

"The scene of what?"

"A murder."

"Don't try to protect me James – tell me everything."

The waiter arrived with steaming dishes which James identified.

"Okay – The next batch of information is a combination of what I know from the Mind Link, and what Pete and I believe were the chain of events. But there are still an awful lot of gaps."

"Carry on, this is fascinating," as she served herself a

97

sampling of each dish.

"Helga sent Pete's father a picture of herself, since she felt the child may bear some resemblance, and I immediately recognized her as the woman I saw your grandfather having lunch with in Mullion."

"This was a Mind Link recollection?"

"Exactly, so if we try and connect the pieces we have so far, we think Pete's father finished the case and sent the results to Helga, she contacted your grandfather who flew to England to meet her. We know he stayed in Mullion as there isn't a Hotel in Cadgewith, and by chance I was there."

Helen lifted a hand, "But, hold on James, you haven't explained why she would contact my grandfather?"

"You're right, I'm sorry. Pete's father discovered that Helga's son was adopted in 1946 by your grandfather."

"My grandfather? Adopted a German baby?"

"Yes… your uncle, Erik Banner."

Chapter 18

For a few terror-filled seconds his mind made the wrenching transition from ignorance to awareness, as he woke at an unknown hour and his sleepy eyes adjusted to the nearby images that seemed to be bathed in a yellow light like old faded photographs. His body felt bent and brutalized by the hard flooring and his empty stomach churned – 'I must get to my feet and move around.

Staggering about at first, he stretched to work out the kinks, "Damn."

His voice was hoarse, and mouth dry. Reaching for a water bottle he finished half of it and recklessly poured the remainder over his head and neck, wiping away the drips from his face with his forearm, threw the empty container irritably and swept both hands through his hair.

His eyes felt dry and his vision milky, as he continued to adjust to the extreme contrast in light levels between the lamp and the pitch-black area beyond its reach.

"AH!" he shouted, spying another buoy bobbing in the water. Dragging it out, he sat down before opening the chest and checking its contents. "Two waters, two dozen food drinks – Ah ha, good, a fresh kerosene canister and matches, three more weights, and... and... no bloody communication!"

James tipped the contents out alongside his other provisions and in a fit of temper kicked the empty chest and sent it flying across the pool of water, "Well, if you bastards think the silent treatment will make me more cooperative, you've got another think coming."

The floating chest wobbled, keeled over, and began to take on water. This additional weight flipped it completely over so it released air bubbles from the now immersed sides. He paid this no attention at first, but then... something? Abruptly sitting up straight, he stared intently at the chest and muttered, "Of course... the smuggler."

It was not so much a humorous story as a clever one, in that it epitomized the cunning art of diversion. If anyone other than his father had told him the drollery James would most likely have forgotten it soon after – but loss of a loved one makes you preserve even the most trivial of memories. It seemed funny though, that it should come back to him now.

A guiding light had miraculously reached this Godforsaken pit, and with renewed zeal James worked indefatigably using the items at hand.

'Now, these nylon cords are about three feet in length... fifteen strands each, so that will give me about three forty-five-foot lines... no, make it two sixty-foot guidelines... that's good...'

The story involved a man who crossed the border every day carrying a bail of straw in a wheelbarrow. The border agent suspected he was smuggling and so insisted the bail was opened so he could inspect every individual flake...

'Each of these containers is about six cubic feet, and I'll probably use about half of that, or more, in placement... but then I should be fine on small parts of carbon dioxide for a while.'

As years passed the frustrated agent watched as the man became rich, but he could never find anything hidden in any of the bails of straw. Years later, when they had both retired and met by chance in a pub, the ex-agent pleaded with the man to tell him what he had smuggled across the border...

'I'll put the first just at the outer reaches of visible range, which is at about thirty feet, and so that will give me a total of... a hundred and fifty feet.'

Smiling in reply, the border-crossing man bought the ex-agent a drink, raised his glass, and answered – wheelbarrows!

James had finished his preparations, and smiled to himself – 'You underestimated the importance of the container...'

He knew the execution of this escape was fraught with danger, and so before starting he sat down, snapped off a sharp stalagmite, and carefully etched out on a flat slab the details of his plan, hoping to convince himself the odds were in his favor.

'"Descartes step one – Never accept anything as true unless it is clear and distinct enough to exclude all doubt from your mind." Right, well let's just hope they're trying to intimidate me, because if it's two hundred feet long I can just make it... But, if it is in fact two hundred yards... then this is all for nothing.

'"Descartes step two – Divide the problem into as many parts as necessary, in order to find a solution." See if I can get more light into the tunnel, position the chests, evaluate the grade to see how far I will have to swim up when out.

'"Descartes step three – Start with the simplest tasks and then tackle the complex." New chests will have to be pushed into position, and that will probably require several dives. Once in position, I'll use them as waypoints... then, attach cords to handles, and repeat from the new vantage point.

'"Descartes step four – Review the solution so generally and completely to be sure nothing was omitted." Huh... I don't even want to begin listing the flaws... but it is viable, and... it's all I've got.'

Chapter 19

The limousine glided through security gates of the Banner estate, parked under the covered entrance and Erik Banner exited. Entering the kitchen, he filled a cup with coffee from the urn and entered the drawing room. Helen was relaxing on a loveseat reading a book and on seeing her he turned to leave.

"Please don't leave."

"I wouldn't want to disturb you – I can use the study."

"No, please – I would welcome the chance to talk."

Reluctantly he obliged, sitting in an armchair opposite, placing his coffee on a side table and removing a financial statement from his briefcase. "Maybe we could postpone the chat as I have a budget meeting in about an hour."

"I have a few questions," she replied with annoyance.

"Would you mind if I read as we talk?"

"No."

"So what's on your mind?"

"I was doing a little research online, and I'm a little confused about Granddad and Mom."

Only half listening, "Why?"

"Well, for instance, what was Granddad doing in England at that time, and…"

"Vacationing."

"And, how did Mom drown in the pool? She was a high school water polo champion."

"What brought this up?"

"I was just interested and you were older at the time so I hoped you could help me understand a little better."

"She was on heavy tranquilizers after hearing of your grandfather's death – the coroner said she must have slipped and struck her head."

"It didn't seem a little strange to you at the time?"

"No, you're Mom was pretty cut up about the accident. I had an apartment downtown at the time and was considering a partnership in Elbers and Finch – I was very distracted."

"But, don't you think…"

Lowering his report irritably to his lap, "No I don't."

Resuming her book, "Well, thank you for your help."

Collecting his things to leave. "It doesn't appear to be helping, this psychology hobby of yours – What about a more practical, less self-indulgent pursuit?"

"Why are you attacking me? Why can't we ever discuss anything pleasantly?"

"You may have the time for this – I don't," Erik replied, rising.

"What do you know of Helga Hawthorne?"

The coffee mug slipped out of his hand and he stepped back quickly to avoid the resulting splash. "Have the Mexican woman clean this up, will you."

Shaking with rage. "You mean, Maria."

"I mean the house cleaner."

"A mask is sometimes more revealing than a face – for that which hides also reveals."

As he left the room he called back, "I don't know what that means, Helen, and I don't want it explained to me."

**

Seeing Helen's car pull into the driveway James walked out to greet her closing the front door behind him – something was wrong.

"What is it, Helen?"

"Am I late?"

"No, we're not expected for half an hour, and it's a ten-minute walk. Now what's wrong?"

"I've just done something stupid."

"Do you want to come in for a while?"

"No, let's walk."

James put his arm around her and he could feel the tension. "Tell me what happened."

"I saw Erik this afternoon – he lives at his North County ranch, but uses the house as it's closer for downtown meetings. Well, after what you told me, I just haven't been able to get it out of my mind."

"I know what you mean."

"It doesn't make sense. I know Pete thinks there's a connection between his father's death and my grandfather but I don't... and anyway, why would anybody kill someone over a mother trying to track down her long lost son?"

"I agree, it's confusing."

"Exactly, and so when I saw Erik, I thought he might clear this whole thing up."

"And was he helpful?"

"No... he was his usual self."

"Did he shed any light?"

"No, he irritated me. So, I asked him about Helga."

"And?"

"I got his attention."

"But he didn't answer the question?"

"No, I told him her name was mentioned in one of the articles I found... but I could kick myself for it now."

"Why? I honestly don't think it matters."

"Maybe you're right – I just hate it when he gets the better of me like that."

"Now let me distract you... Pete called me just before you arrived."

"Any news?"

"Yes, he spoke to a detective in Helston, which is the closest police station to Mullion and Cadgewith, and he was very helpful."

"Good."

"It seems your grandfather's case was linked to a second case."

"What?"

"A missing person's report filed the following day."

"Don't tell me... Helga Hawthorne?"

"Yes. Her husband, Colin, had taken his fishing boat out on the evening tide and when he returned the following morning she had disappeared."

"Why would they have suspected a connection between my grandfather and Helga?"

"Colin believed your grandfather had something to do with his wife's disappearance as they had met for lunch earlier, and when she came down to the beach to see him off, she had been very depressed. At the time, the police suspected a love triangle and that Colin had killed them both but the theory was later dropped as his crew and neighbors provided his alibi."

"Did they ever find her?"

"This detective didn't know, but he did give Colin's contact information to Pete, and he has called several times but he just hangs up."

Helen used her fingers as she listed each point. "So, Pete's father is killed soon after he completes a case for Helga... Helga goes missing the day after my grandfather has his accident... and my mother has an accident two days after that. Something was very wrong back then."

"It seems so... did you want to drop this?"

Helen turned in astonishment. "Absolutely not. What else did Pete have to say?"

"He thinks I should go to England to see Colin."

Helen turned in excitement. "He didn't want to go?"

With a smile he replied, "He said it would be better if I go because I know how to drive on the wrong side of the road, and speak the same strange language!"

"I hope you didn't let him get away with that?"

"No... I taught him the famous Olde English tongue twister – WHALE OIL BEEF HOOKED – and told him the faster he could say it the more it would improve his pronunciation."

Helen paused for a moment in concentration, then attempted it herself with increasing speed, "Whale oil beef hooked, whale oil beef hooked," then stopped and laughed when she realized what she was really saying. "He's probably still walking around the station muttering it to himself!"

Stopping, he pulled her towards him. "Helen, I don't suppose..."

"Yes."

Chapter 20

Erik Banner hurried from a downtown restaurant to his waiting limousine – it was late evening and his suit and hair were buffeted by a brisk wind that had just picked up. The business dinner had delayed him longer than he wanted and as he walked he opened his briefcase, glanced inside, and then with unaccustomed irritation slammed it shut.

"To the ranch, sir?" questioned his driver, opening the door as he approached.

"Yes," he replied curtly, climbing into the car and settling himself alongside Karl who cut short a telephone conversation. The limousine pulled smoothly into the late-evening traffic.

"Well?"

"A surveillance team will be monitoring her 24/7, and research teams have been assigned."

"What have they found so far?"

Referring to a laptop, Karl replied, "She's lying. There is no reference to Helga in any articles on her mother or grandfather – we get no results on a search of her name."

"Who's the source then?"

"I'll know shortly."

"Good – where is she this evening?"

Pointing to the computer monitor and using the cursor control, Karl read a report that had digital photographs alongside text. "She left the Banner Estate at 6:17, drove directly to this residence, the home of a James Moore. They talked for twelve minutes outside the house, walked three blocks, embraced, and then walked to this house. Research have determined the people greeting them in this photograph are a Paul and Sheryl Barnes. They had dinner, and stayed for just over three hours."

"And then what?"

Scrolling down the report, Karl points out several long-range shots through house windows showing the four of them having dinner together, and openly enjoying each other's company. The next several shots show James and Helen saying good bye to their hosts and getting progressively more affectionate as they walk down the street.

"Did an electronics unit get in while they were gone?"

"No."

"And why not?"

"His home security system is extremely sophisticated. They will need more time to be able to gain access."

Erik leaned forward and focused his attention on a photograph of James. "What do we know about this man?"

Extracting a printed page from a file in his briefcase, Karl replied, "Preliminary information only at this time – full name, James Edward Moore, thirty-four years old, originally from England, has been in the US for ten years, became a US. Citizen, teaches at the university, has a Federally funded grant to develop a biological computer, has published several textbooks, and holds many technology patents."

"I want a detailed brief on all these people, and anyone else she comes in contact with."

"We should report this breach?"

"NO. I will deal with it."

"Conflict?"

Erik returned Karl's stare. "What are they doing now?"

"They are in the Moore house. Surveillance had to switch to infrared and move to high ground to get an angle on the rear of the house... I can show you a live feed?"

"Go ahead."

Karl selected an icon in the continually updating report, and at first the video was a grainy-green with range/angle readouts in the upper corner, a target reticule in the center, and the word 'rec' flashing at the bottom right. It appeared to be shot through a bedroom window showing at first a heat signature and then a recognizable near naked male and female body intertwined, leaning up against a wall kissing passionately. The video switched to an extreme close-up that identified Helen's head tilting back in ecstasy and biting her bottom lip as James drops to his knees. The audio came in, intermittent at first, and then they could hear the unmistakable moans of a man and woman making love. The video now showed Helen's nails digging deep into James' shoulder, and she pulled him up, pushed him onto the bed, crawled on top of him, kissed his neck and chest and slowly moved down his body.

Erik reached over and slammed the laptop shut, and in a raised voice said, "Move that man back, immediately."

Karl turned towards him, his eyes a startling blue in his pallid face. "This should be dealt with."

Chapter 21

"I wondered where you'd gone," Helen asked sleepily, walking up behind James, slipping her arms around him and resting her head on his back. The light in the kitchen was dim, enhancing a feeling of intimacy.

"I didn't want to wake you."

"What time is it?"

"Around two."

Turning and leaning against the counter, James pulled Helen into his arms. Her hair was tousled and she was wearing one of his sweatshirts – she felt warm and inviting. Pushing his hands under the sweatshirt and caressing her back, he kissed her neck gently and moved slowly up to her lips.

Leaning in to him, Helen reached up and ran her fingers through his hair. "I know you've been trying to protect me but you mustn't – I want to know."

Helen seated herself at the breakfast table and watched as James set up the Mind Link.

Taking a seat adjacent, he initialized the system and tried once again. "You shouldn't see this."

"I insist, James."

Placing a headset on her. "This is the repeater… this is your grandfather, for heaven's sake!"

"All the more reason."

"You realize this is irreversible – it haunted me for days."

Helen narrowed her eyes in defiance.

James placed the primary headset on himself, activated the system and their present view blinked, collapsed, and they were all at once enveloped in a coastal image. Helen could see a rocky path running alongside a rugged coastline, and a few white puffy clouds in an otherwise clear blue sky. Then, a sense of awareness came over her and she could sense the sun's warmth, the seagulls cry, and the smell of salt from the sea. She marveled at the clarity and found herself captivated by otherwise mundane details such as the wind lifting seeds from the heather along the hedgerows.

She realized this was going nowhere and knew James was hesitating, and so she reached out her hand blindly, found his shoulder and moved down to his hand and squeezed it reassuringly.

The scene flipped to show a young James approaching his father, who was relaxing on a hotel patio with a pot of coffee and the morning newspaper. Leaning forward his father brushes back James' hair and kisses him on the forehead. "Go on then, but don't be long – and please be careful."

Helen heard the young James reply as he ran off. "Thanks, Dad."

He ran down a set of steps carved into the cliff to an empty cove, and once at the base began to climb up the cliffs face. Helen was surprised at the level of danger and tensed along with the young James as he strained and slipped his way to a ledge just below the cliff ridge. She got the distinct impression the young James was playing 'Cowboys and Indians' when he saw a man approaching through a small gap in the rocks and ducked down into a hidden position, but then slowly lifted himself back up to spy the man approaching.

Helen recognized him instantly as her grandfather, around sixty-five, distinguished, and dressed in a tweed jacket and peaked cap he carried a walking stick and frequently stopped to use binoculars. Now almost upon him the young James was surprised by a second person, who had concealed himself behind a set of rocks and as he looked up, he could see his feet and a sharp piece of slate rock in his hand.

Apparently unseen by Hugh Banner, the assailant stepped out quickly and with a fully extended discus-like arm swung the rock so that it sliced across his face lifting him off his feet and sending him with a thud to the ground. The young James ducked down shaking uncontrollably, breathing rapidly, pressed himself tight against the rock face, and closed his eyes.

A thump caused the young James to look up and see the bloodied and beaten face of Banner who now hung just over the edge, staring down at James. He shuddered and uttered the words 'Help me', and Helen heard the young James mute an involuntary faint cry and as he tried to back away he almost fell.

A rock came down violently from behind to deliver a death blow to the back of the head and blood showered on James, and then the body was heaved over the side.

The Link collapsed and James quickly removed the headsets to hold a desperately sobbing Helen in his arms.

For quite some time Helen was understandably inconsolable, but it was when she had calmed and still in James' arms she felt his body tense, and looked up to see him puzzled. "What is it, James?"

"I'm not sure, love… Come with me." He led her into the hall where he stopped and pulled her against the wall.

"James, what?"

"Hold on, Helen. Butler, switch kitchen monitor to display family room and kitchen only. What is the security status?"

"Display switched. All perimeter sensors are inactive. Home

secure. The only motion is from where I am receiving your voice commands, sir."

"James, you're scaring me."

"When we were in the kitchen, I was distracted by a bright beam of light that appeared on the security monitor."

"I didn't see anything."

"No, you'd only have seen it if you were watching the monitor."

"I... don't understand."

"Somebody is out there using an infrared night vision system. The infrared light is invisible to us, but not to the video cameras."

Helen looked down the hallway as if expecting to see someone appear. "Yes, but..."

Seeing her anxious gaze. "This person's just watching Helen, and it must be from the front of the house."

Crouching down, he guided her through to the office. Rummaging through a large desk drawer he grabbed a strange looking pair of binoculars, knelt down under the front-facing window, and used them to look down the length of the street.

"Those are weird looking," she whispered.

"Modified for night vision."

"But surely, if you detected them, then they'll be able to see you?"

"Mine is passive – there's is active... Ah, a car, and the silhouette of two men. Helen, without getting up, see if you can reach a pencil and pad off my desk."

"Okay, I've got it."

"It's an SUV, and they're at an angle, I can't see the number. Butler, call Pete's cell."

Several rings sounded before Pete answered in a sleepy

voice, "Yes?"

"Pete, it's me James, there's…"

Pete interrupted. "What's this, English time? It is in fact 2:50 a.m.!"

James altered his tone. "Pete, listen, there's two men here in a car watching with night surveillance equipment."

Now fully awake. "Okay, don't panic, just stay calm and don't panic."

"I'm not."

"I'll call it in right now, you should see several squad cars in less than two minutes – I'll be there in ten."

After Pete had hung up, James sat down with his back to the wall and Helen huddled next to him. Interrupted by the sound of a car engine starting, they both peered over the window ledge to see the vehicle make a sharp screeching turn and disappear into the night.

Chapter 22

James had noticed that clothes just didn't seem to hang right on Pete. Whenever they had met during the day, he had always been distracted by his consistently unkempt appearance. It was three a.m., and James and Helen had dressed; the police had taken a report and left, and the three of them sat in the living room with a tray of coffee on the table in front of them. Once again, James found himself diverted from his train of thought by Pete's attire, which on this occasion had reached new depths of disheveled slovenliness. The wisps of thinning hair encircling his head stretched out uncontrolled in all directions. He was wearing a pair of leather strapped sandals revealing one dark brown and one black sock, an aging pair of navy-blue corduroy trousers, stretched and bagging at the knees, and a plain off-white T shirt. In an attempt to improve his appearance, he had finished off this ensemble with a smart gray-blue jacket. "That's a nice jacket, Pete."

"Thanks, bought it six years ago. It's odd, but everyone compliments me on it – and you know the funny thing, it only cost me twelve dollars," he said proudly producing a tatty receipt from the top pocket and handing it to James.

This was not a receipt to be proud of – for although it did indeed confirm the jacket had only cost twelve dollars, it also revealed it had been bought from a Thrift Store.

James handed Pete back the receipt, whereupon it was carefully folded and returned to the top pocket in preparation for the next admirer.

"So you think this is connected?" Helen asked.

"I'm certain of it." Taking a sip of his coffee he noticed anxiety cross her face, and so added, "They made a mistake here this evening and almost got caught. I'm goin' to make a big noise about this and get some resources to track 'em down."

"Thanks for getting here so quickly Pete. Helen and I were thinking of maybe leaving earlier for England. Get out of here for a while."

"I think that's a damned good idea. When can you leave?"

"Helen has classes 'til the end of this week, I have a quick two-day business trip and will be back by Friday, so we thought we'd leave this weekend."

"The fewer people you tell the better."

"Any new information, Pete?"

"Not much. I found out Helga's maiden name was Kluge, and she was born in Frankfurt. I've tried Colin Hawthorne's phone number a few more times, but no joy."

***

With unnecessary opulence and ornate splendor, The Regal restaurant on Coronado Island was occupied by the usual elegantly dressed couples all exuding the appearance of wealth and an entitled air. Off to one side in a cordoned off private dining area, Erik Banner sat opposite a beautiful woman in a deep-blue gown. Aesthetically pleasing to the eye she contributed nothing to the conversation and only smiled projecting an image of synthetic enjoyment. When a reporter, escorted by the maitre d', arrived at the table's edge requesting a photograph of the couple, Erik initially objected to the intrusion unconvincingly and then conceded graciously.

Entering the restaurant, Karl positioned himself to catch Erik's eye as he modestly answered questions about being one of America's most eligible bachelors. Having seen Karl beckon, he excused himself from his companion and the journalist to join Karl in a vacant seating area adjacent to the bar.

"I have the missing link you requested."

"Good."

"At 2:07 this morning, our surveillance unit abandoned their task after being detected."

"What! Are you employing amateurs?"

"On the contrary – we underestimated a professional. Discovering he was being monitored, Mr. Moore called the police, control picked up the dispatch and recalled our unit."

"How did he know?"

"I have the police report – it's quite ingenious as to how he discovered them."

"Anything more on this guy?

Opening a manila folder and scanning a page. "Yes – Former Royal Navy officer, electronic warfare specialist, received the Distinguished Service Order during the Falklands War... All of this, however, is beside the point."

"Then be so kind as to make your point?"

"An item at the end of the police report that mentions the arrival of a homicide detective."

"What has Homicide got to do with this?"

"Mr. Moore and the detective appear to be friends."

"What's the name of this detective?"

"Pete Hammond." Knowing that this piece of information would need to be digested, Karl waited.

"Hammond?"

"Yes. This is his son, and I believe the source."

"How much do they know?"

"More than they should."

"Take care of this, Karl."

"Including Helen?"

Tapping his hand against his thigh, Erik stared at Karl, his expression unreadable. The silence was palpable and tension filled the air. Karl proceeded forcefully, "The Fahnenbrueder must be informed."

Stepping forward and turning his head to one side to conceal a look of rage he moved to within inches of Karl's face, and in a biting tone snapped, "DON'T... PUSH... ME."

Chapter 23

James leaned his forehead against the aircraft's window staring down as San Diego's landmarks eventually appeared uninhabited. Banking west and leveling out, the plane passed through a cumulus cloud layer that obscured the topography below making it seem as though they were suspended, motionless in a pale blue sky. Enjoying the peace and solitude he selected the reclined position and decided to take a leisurely snooze.

"Refreshment, sir?" asked a stewardess.

James had accepted after many years of trans-Atlantic flights that all airlines were incapable of making a decent cup of coffee. "Orange juice please."

"Business trip?"

"I'm afraid so… just a couple of days."

She handed him his drink, "Don't work too hard."

"I'll certainly try not to!"

Across the aisle a round-faced man with thick brown hair beamed a smile. In his early forties, he was short and stocky, wearing a sky-blue polyester suit and bright tie. "You and me both, buddy."

This was something James always dreaded – getting trapped with a talkative stranger on a long flight. He had seen the man bustling on board at the last moment, his overstuffed hand luggage banging against his shins, and hoped against hope his assigned seat was as far from him as possible – especially as the business cabin was half empty. But, alas, he plonked himself opposite, huffing and puffing loudly as he stuffed his bags in the overhead compartment.

James responded with a smile, and tried to send a signal by resuming his nap.

"What line of business you in?"

"Teaching." James paused and then added reluctantly, "And you?"

As he spoke, he arranged his chubby hands like a tent, fingertip to fingertip, bouncing them off each other. "Aerospace executive – I always travel professional class. Yep, the job demands a lot of my time which is probably why my wife left me for some blue-collar jerk – Caught 'em in bed together and they gave her custody of the kids... Richard Jacobs - m' friends call me Dick."

"Oh dear, that's a shame." James knew this response was sorely inadequate but it had always shocked him when people he hardly knew divulged such personal information right off the bat.

"It's not the first time it's happened. Been married twice, two kids from both... I guess I'm just not that good a husband."

"Oh, I'm sure that's not true..." James' discomfiture was now at an all-time high. This was too much – first he was made privy to intimate details of this man's marriage, and now he had somehow been cornered into the position of counselor. Refusing to go any further until certain formalities had been dealt with, he lifted himself slightly from his seat and stretched out his hand. "James Moore."

"As I said, m' friends call me Dick. Here, have one of my business cards – just been promoted, Jim."

"Good for you. Do you have a connecting flight in Oahu?"

"No, I'm stayin' in Honolulu. We have a division there and I guess they gotta major problem... which is where I come in."

"Oh, I see. Well, best of luck with that."

"What are you goin' to be doin', Jim?"

"Well, a professor at the University of Hawaii is considering one of my textbooks for adoption. He called my editor to see if I could give a guest lecture to the faculty during their spring break in-service."

"So, you're a book writer. Good for you. I like action movies. Have you written any action movies?"

"No... You see, I write textbooks, for teaching."

"Oh... What about war movies – done any war movies?"

"No, my books cover electronic engineering and mathematics."

"Not a lot of excitement in those then."

"No... I suppose not."

"So where are you stayin', Jim?"

James clenched his teeth, "The Marriott?"

"Ah, that's a bummer. I'm at the Best Western."

Holding back a sigh of relief. "Oh dear, that is a shame."

"I'm goin' to be renting a car, you want me to drop you off."

"No, that's okay, but thank you. This professor is meeting me at the airport."

"Well, if you're ever in Denver look me up. Maybe we could catch a ball game and have a couple of beers!"

Chapter 24

Police headquarters was in the Gas-lamp area of downtown San Diego, just off Harbor drive. Set back from the road behind a stonewall and an open wrought iron double gateway, the large Spanish mission-style building was both impressive and pleasing to the eye. Its façade was long, solid and symmetrical, and above the second floor a pitched red-tiled roof reared up either side to a central pediment topped by an ornate clock tower.

At seven a.m. on a cold and gloomy Friday morning the usual confusion of people moved in and out of the large double door entrance, corralled somewhat into an orderly pattern by barriers. Pete drove his old and badly weathered Chevy Nova into the parking lot, flashed his badge at the officer at the security gate, and proceeded down to the underground parking area and into his designated space. A group of uniformed officers stood talking near several patrol cars and their conversation stopped momentarily as Pete exited his car and ambled towards the elevator.

"Morning Pete, how you doin'?" called out one.

"Good, Dave… and you?" Pete muttered, waving his hand, but not stopping to hear the reply. Wearing faded worn jeans, a padded jacket and a woolen hat he looked more like a vagrant than a detective. Tiredly running a hand across his face and his raspy stubble, he strolled to the elevator and pressed the call button.

"C'mon, c'mon." Finally, after hearing a few good-natured

shouts and the slamming of car doors, the patrol cars started up and departed, leaving a trail of fumes in their wake. Pete was at last alone in the dank expanse of this concrete cave and in their absence the underground parking lot seemed echoey and cold. Stretching his shoulders and rolling his head he tried in vain to release a knot in the muscles of his back. Shoving his hands in his pockets he leaned his shoulder up against the wall as he waited.

He sensed more than saw a shadow and turned quickly to face a heavy-set, youngish man with a walrus mustache and no neck, wearing a maintenance overall and a baseball cap with the word "Padres" emblazoned across the front. Pete glared at him as he opened up the elevator's control panel to expose the circuitry. He said nothing.

"I guess this means you want me to take the stairs."

"No need. This is only routine."

"So it's working?"

"Yep." The man shrugged indifferently and as the doors opened to the accompaniment of a loud "ding", Pete crossed into the cab just hesitating long enough to look down thoughtfully at the man kneeling in front of the open access panel.

Once inside he shook his head dismissing any sinister notion, pressed the '2'-button, and the doors closed. A long delay ensued before the elevator responded, the silence and emptiness fueling an irrational premonition. This apprehension was reinforced when the cab shuddered and dropped fractionally before gaining an upward momentum.

His heightened level of awareness seemed to amplify his senses. Could he really smell the acrid odor of an electric fire? Was that snap he heard, the hauling cables being strained beyond their tension limit? When the cab came to a grinding halt just short of the second floor, he had convinced himself of the worst and was pressing several buttons to no avail.

The cab creaked menacingly and as he looked down at his feet, he was, all at once, reminded of a story a maternal uncle had imparted when he was a youth. Uncle Joey had been a crane operator his entire working life and shortly before retirement a major support cable gave way and the whole structure came tumbling down. In those seconds before impact Joey described how his deceased mother had appeared and told him to get his feet off the floor. Hospitalized for several months, Uncle Joey miraculously survived the three hundred-foot fall, largely in part the experts believe, because he climbed up the walls of his control booth and so was spared the full force of the impact.

With this memory flooding back to him Pete slowly backed into a corner, put one foot on a side rail and placed his other foot on the adjacent wall's rail. In this spread-eagled position he pressed his outstretched arms against the walls for further support, and tilted his head to one side due to the low ceiling. His arms began to burn with the strain as he pressed hard against the walls to prevent himself falling forward, and his splayed-out legs felt numb.

It was at this inopportune moment the elevator impulsively lurched upwards to complete its passage and the doors opened to reveal several waiting colleagues. At first they stared speechless at the spectacle of Pete plastered up against the wall in this ungainly position, but this quickly broke into uncontrolled laughter.

Hopping down as nonchalantly as he could, he exited the elevator and hurried out and in response to the cat calls barked, "Haven't you assholes seen yoga before?"

Red-faced and humiliated he weaved his way between the

desks of the Homicide Department, snatched up the phone on his desk and slapped the operator button.

"Maintenance, Dan here."

"This is detective Hammond, can you tell the idiot working on the elevators to shut 'em down if they're busted."

A gruff voice replied, "No one's working on the elevators."

"Then who the hell was the guy I saw in the parking garage fucking with the panel?"

"I dunno... routine maintenance isn't scheduled for weeks."

"Right, I'm going to check, and if you're lying you're in deep shit."

"Go ahead and knock yourself out," came the affronted reply.

Slamming down the phone, Pete leapt out of his seat and rushed out of the office oblivious of the silent stares following him. Using the stairs, he searched high and low hoping to catch the hapless technician, and after a wasted hour conceded defeat and returned to his desk slumping into his chair.

Sam Patterson, a veteran detective and a good friend of his late father, sat at the desk opposite calmly reading a report. With a gentle well-rounded amused face, hooded eyes and a thin down of white hair, he gave off an air of inner tranquility. Peering up and over his half-lens reading glasses perched on the end of his nose he took a sip of coffee from an oversized mug and said calmly, "Bad day, Pete?"

"No... I almost got killed in the elevator."

"Oh my."

"Sam, there was some guy messing with the elevator, and it starts tripping out on the way up. And now nobody knows any elevator guy... I think that's weird."

"They had electricians up here earlier... it was probably one

125

of them."

"Well, why didn't dip-shit Dan tell me that?"

"You were too busy being rude."

Leaning back into his chair deflated, Pete unraveled a paper clip and began to pick at an already well-worked hole in his desk. "Everything is fucked up."

Sam did not respond.

"The Captain pulled me in to give an update on the Smithfield case. What a crock... I get my work done."

"Except when you're working on that Hawthorne case."

"What are you talking about?"

Sam removed his glasses, put his paperwork down, and fixed a solemn stare on Pete. "I work on the books for Judy's antique store, Jerry does his boy-scout stuff, it doesn't matter as long as you don't overdo it – tell the Captain what you want, but don't bullshit me."

"You're right, I'm sorry."

"Is that why you're so uptight?"

"Yeah... I don't get it."

"Stop being so hard on everyone... especially yourself. Your Dad and I were partners for fifteen years and we went through some crap together. Come over tonight and let me take a look at what you got."

"Thanks, Sam."

"Don't worry about it – we all fuck up."

"Including Dad?"

Sam chuckled, "He was a master at it... I miss him."

"Me too."

Chapter 25

Even the air seemed to smell of darkness, in spite of the newly fueled lamp burning at maximum brilliance. An icicle-shaped stalagmite had easily cut through the cans and by wedging them into the lamp's grill James had fashioned a crude but effective parabola that better directed the luminous energy into the watery tunnel. He could feel its heat on his cheek and at this burn rate he would almost certainly run out of fuel before being resupplied – 'No light and no heat… don't think about it.'

Sealing one of the chests he pushed and kicked it as deep into the tunnel as he could, snatched a lungful of air and went under. Grabbing the chest's handle, he wrestled it away from the ceiling and pulled it with him, fighting its natural buoyancy – 'Good, the light extends almost twice as far. I can put this one much farther than I planned.'

At about forty feet the curved ceiling of the lava tube was still just visible and so he let the chest rise up and settle against the tunnel's apex. His lungs were beginning to protest as he grappled with the handles, released the catches, and watched as some air escaped as the lid and a single diving-weight dropped to the floor – 'Use two weights in the other chests to cut down on the resistance of getting them into position.'

Surfacing inside the chest he could not be sure if he was within an air pocket – 'I don't have enough air to get back… I can't tell… How can I tell?'

Holding on until the pain was unbearable, he involuntarily

opened his mouth and let out a guttural yell before violently inhaling… and to his utter relief, his cry echoed back hollowly in the inverted pressurized chest. For quite some time he hyper-ventilated seeing stars flash up against a blood red backing in the pitch-black interior of the chest – '…thank God, it works.'

The trapped air jammed the chest hard against the upper limit of the tunnel and it wouldn't budge even when he held the sides and gave it his full weight – 'Leave quickly, this first staging point will be most frequently used.'

Taking a deep breath, he ducked down and returned to the entrance, climbed out, and shook his head in reproach. "That was stupid, snap your fingers – that'll tell whether its air or water… and don't push out so far, I must have enough to get back."

Hearing his own voice helped. Grabbing a nylon cord he tied the end to a second chest and coiled the remaining length, sealed two weights within it and returned to the water's edge.

The process from here on was long and laborious but he continued to make good progress. With the loose end of the cord tied to the established first air-pocket chest he carted the sealed chest forward, systematically leaving it at new vantage points along the way and returning for air using the cord as a return guide.

He discovered several unforeseen factors actually worked in his favor in that the partially buoyant sealed chests would bob up naturally to the ceiling's high point and this helped him to navigate deeper down into the now pitch-black tunnel. It was slow, exhausting work, and he had to double back four times before the cord was taut and the second air-pocket chest was in place. He also found the more acclimatized he got to this dark underwater world, the more relaxed he became and the longer his oxygen would last.

There was of course a downside, and unexpected problems arose, but luckily he was quick to adapt and compensate. As expected, the first chest's air supply was quickly depleted due to over use, and the higher ratio of carbon dioxide to oxygen made him quite light headed. He refreshed the reservoir by holding a buoy directly beneath the chest and piercing it with the sharp stalagmite. With his head in the chest, the fresh bubbles billowed up and splashed him in the face and he could almost taste the fresh air and feel his head clear as the oxygen was replenished.

It was when he was moving ahead autonomously on the third leg, about twenty feet out from the second staging point, he first sensed warmth in the water. He initially rejected the sensation, putting it down to exertion but as he pressed on it was unmistakable – 'Stay calm.'

It was difficult to curb an impulsive urge to drop everything, take a deep breath, and charge forward in hopes of reaching the lava tube's end. Heading back to recharge his oxygen he returned with renewed vigor to drag the chest forward until the cord was tight and set the final air pocket.

Sucking in several deep breaths he looked forward to see the dim blue-green circle of the tunnel's end – 'It's too far? Damn, about twenty-five feet, maybe thirty… and the grade of the tube? How far do I have to swim up? I need air.'

Surfacing in the chest he deliberated out loud. "Based on the angle of slope I'd say I'm sixty feet down. So that's thirty out and sixty up… that's too far, it's much too far. Extend the chest? you'll lose too much air. I need more options."

Dropping down and swimming forward he panicked when the light at the aperture of the tube appeared to eclipse – a diver!

Instinctively, he pulled himself out of sight and watched as the scuba diver placed another buoy and chest just inside the tube's entrance and left.

Pulling up into the chest to refresh his air, he exhaled and inhaled – 'Oh bloody hell, I'm feeling lightheaded again.'

Dropping down he watched the chest moving towards him in a pendulum-like action – 'Wait… a little longer.'

Lifting up once more into the chest he snatched another breath and then swam forward like a man possessed towards the new chest. His vision was the first to be impaired as the carbon dioxide began to poison his system but adrenalin coursed through his veins overriding the toxic effects.

On reaching the new chest he grabbed it's handles, twisted it upside down, released the side catches, and was dragged up to the ceiling of the tube while being showered with the contents. The moment the chest thumped against the upper surface he pulled his head up and into the fresh air reservoir.

***

Jutting out into the ocean majestically, the beach was covered in black sand bordered by thick tropical rainforests that abruptly ended at heavily lava-scarred green grass fields that rose dramatically to a high snowcapped mountain peak. The diversity of the island was magnificent with the seasons represented at different altitudes.

The diver surfaced at the rear of a sport-fishing powerboat and clambered aboard.

A man at the helm called out to him, "Okay?"

The diver signaled back with a thumbs up.

Deep down below James took in several deep breaths before ducking down. As he cleared the mouth of the tunnel the sun's refracted light saturated his unaccustomed eyes. His kicks and pulls were orderly at first but soon replaced with panic-driven strokes – 'I can't see.'

A mounting sense of urgency enveloped him as oxygen starved lungs caused his chest to hurt, head to pound, and muscles to numb – 'Swim, swim!'

It was no good, iridescent light filtered through the water creating sparkling stars that seemed to encircle him, and he stopped – 'I give up… sleep.' And then, the voice, clear, and yet distant.

"Less haste…" His father had said this following a surfing wipeout that had sucked him under and twisted and turned him into complete disorientation. He had swum frantically only to find himself at the sea floor. The shallow water on that occasion had been more forgiving, but he had still returned to the shore in tears.

Suspended and motionless in the pose of a free-falling skydiver, an air bubble escaped from his nose and caught his eye as it traveled up at an unexpected angle… and then all at once he was back on the beach in the arms of his father. "James, remember. Less haste, more speed… Float first, and remember bubbles always go up."

Breaching through the surface he gulped down a huge breath and slammed back into the water with a resounding slap. Swallowing some salt water, he gagged and spluttered until his throat was clear, and then rolled onto his back and floated, rising and falling as he sensed his father's spirit departing.

On the deck of the powerboat, the diver stopped stowing his gear and lifted his head unsure as to whether he heard something above the drone of the engine, and as he turned his head, he was revealed as Richard (call me Dick) Jacobs. Calling out to the man at the helm, Dick slid a finger across his throat, and in response the engine was shut off. Jacobs climbed up to the deck, and searched the surrounding sea.

The peaks and valleys of the ocean's swell seemed to be timed miraculously to conceal the floating James. The surface layer was warm and soothing and with his face soaking up the sun and the rest of his body partially submerged, he didn't hear the speedboat engine start up and leave.

Having recuperated, he saw the shore was about half a mile off, and set off settling into a slow rhythmic freestyle stroke.

Chapter 26

The Mexican border town of Tijuana catered to its rich neighbor with elaborate pristine shopping centers that were in stark contrast to the shanty-style homes in the nearby residential district. Tucked in amongst these dilapidated dwellings was the law office of Carlos Ruiz – a true servant of the people. The only feature that distinguished this humble wooden structure from its neighbors was a shingle hung from a wrought iron bar near the porch, bearing his name and occupation.

Slightly built and in his mid-fifties, his face wore the permanent tired expression of a warrior, who had spent too many years fighting an uphill battle against more resourceful opponents. It was about eight p.m. when he locked the office door and strolled to his car, briefcase in hand, reading an article in the Tijuana Gazette. His thick dark hair was ruffled and his brown suit crumpled from being seated most of the day. The dingy street was empty of people, and a slight breeze picked up the surface layer of dirt from the road creating small eddies that seemed to be permanently trapped in darkened corners.

Placing his case and the paper on the roof of his car, he searched his pockets for the keys, and it was then he noticed the two men converging on his position. They were dressed in dusty fatigues and approached in a deliberate manner. A tremor of fear ran up his spine. Assessing them as younger and fitter he quickly abandoned an impulse to run and instead opted for negotiation. "Como están ustedes?"

Now in close proximity, their Caucasian coloring was evident so he reverted to English – all the while panic slowly escalating within him. "Good evening, gentlemen, how are you?"

Without answering, the lead man smiled at his accomplice conspiratorially, and then looked back at Carlos with an expression of cold contempt.

"I don't understand. The deal is done – I did everything he asked."

Certain death was upon him – and Carlos knew it. Without pleading or panicking he dropped to his knees, closed his eyes, clasped his hands, and began to pray fervently.

This easy acceptance of his fate seemed to detract from the executioner's perverse pleasure and in a flash of temper he removed his gun and without hesitation, spitefully shot Carlos in the head.

***

Police headquarters in Hilo, on the Big Island of Hawaii, was a two-story red brick block building on Kalakaua Avenue. With a flat roof and steel windows, its soulless façade was a stark contrast to the surrounding rows of brightly painted tourist shops with their bark-walls and bamboo-thatched awnings, selling head-bobbing hula dolls, all manner of T-shirts, polyurethaned driftwood clocks and cheap wood tikis.

After his arrival on Hanalei Beach it hadn't been difficult to hitch a ride into town. Given a few improbable looks by the desk sergeant he was eventually escorted to an interrogation room and left by himself to make a phone call. Now dressed in a loaned Hawaiian shirt, shorts and rubber flip-flops, James waited as they connected the call.

"Hammond."

"Pete, it's James, I…"

"…Shit, James. They e-mailed me the report. What the hell happened to you?"

"A ruse, ingenious, and cunning… I was lucky."

He sounded fragile. "Just take it slow."

"They wouldn't have let me out – once they had what they want they would stop sending supplies, and the…"

"What did they want?"

"I don't know."

"What about this Professor?"

"Doesn't exist"

"Helen called."

"Is she okay?"

"Yes, she's fine. She knows nothing of what's happened."

"Good."

"Why good."

"C'mon, Pete. You and I know who's behind this, I think Helen unwittingly tipped our hand when she spoke to Banner… what did she say to you?"

"Has the boat returned?"

"No, they're watching the beach but I'm not sure they believe me."

"Just head back, James. I'll get them to keep me posted."

A nondescript clock just behind him, high up on the wall, chimed the hour.

"James, are you there?"

"Yes… I think Helen and I should go to England as soon as possible."

"Good idea, and get some sleep on the plane."

"Yeah, let's just hope I'm not sitting next to another gormless cretin."

"What's this strange language you use?"

James smiled, "It's called English, Pete, sorry if it's confusing!"

***

The steel border fence followed the changes of the terrain in spite of the difficulties, and on the U. S. side a sedan travelled through the suburban neighborhood. Pulling into the driveway of an older home on a large lot, a middle-aged woman exited the car and collected several grocery bags from the passenger seat. Sensing something wrong, she hurried to the door as several neighborhood dogs began to bark in unison. On entering she was greeted by four sobbing women with children gathered close by and as she hears the distant echoing sound of panicked cries for help a look of dread crossed her face.

Two operatives came bounding down the stairs and the women ran to block their path, pleading in Spanish, but they were quickly swept aside. The operatives go through to a bedroom and were met by three pleading Hispanic men who had been working in this makeshift workshop filled with tools and timber.

Pulling aside a large wooden chest, the two men exposed a hidden passage, and travelled down a set of stairs into clouds of dust and towards the painful hoarse shrieks for help that are now loud and clear.

One of the operatives had been in communication with an earpiece. "Please confirm terminate… understood."

At the bottom of the stairs they could hardly see for the density of airborne dust and a small older Hispanic man emerged, every inch of him coated in dirt. He pleaded with the operatives who were attaching silencers to the muzzle of their nine millimeter Semiautomatic – the cries were now deafening.

"Please senor, give me just a little time, I…"

Removing a flashlight from his belt, one of the operatives ducked his head and disappeared into the tunnel.

The face of the older man flinched with each of the muffled puffing thuds sounds that instantly muted the screams. With tears making tracks down his dirty face he approached a makeshift altar adorned with crosses, flowers, and pictures of patron saints, and lit a candle.

Chapter 27

James had hoped that the weather would have been a little more obliging, but the sky remained obstinately full of dark threatening clouds. The dreary day however, had not dampened Helen's enthusiasm. Trading the unattractive efficiency of the motorway for picturesque winding country roads she could not seem to get enough of the lush full-blown landscape.

Spring had just begun, and the buds on all the trees were bursting through giving the countryside a fresh, burgeoning greenness. Ploughed fields extended as far as the eye could see, with only the occasional farmhouse in sight. Drifts of bluebells swept into open meadows studded with grazing sheep and cows. On either side of the road were waterlogged ditches, bordered by tangled blackberry bushes. Beyond these were small woodlands of oak trees, their gnarled trunks thickly covered with moss and ivy, and their long sweeping branches stretching across the narrow road creating a tunnel through which occasional bursts of sunlight filtered through.

The pastoral scenes were dotted with ancient stone villages, and at around mid-day they stopped for lunch at the Kings Arms, a black-and-white timbered Elizabethan pub with unpretentious charm. The bar was furnished with tapestry-covered settles, old oak refectory tables, and an open fireplace with a copper hood. The walls were covered with paintings of fox-hunting scenes and a variety of horse-brasses. Two elderly men sat – almost motionless – in a small alcove hunched over a chessboard, each holding a pint of beer. Captivated by the olde-worlde charm, Helen took great delight in studying every one of the menu's choices, and eventually decided on James' choice of shepherd's pie.

Traveling along the coastal road past cliff-side farms, James showed Helen Devon's jagged coast from which Drake and Raleigh had set sail and where pirates and smugglers used to find safe haven.

"We're here," announced James, turning up a small road that squeezed its way through two rows of small stone houses. Crossing the town square he turned up a small lane and parked alongside a thatched cottage.

"It's beautiful," Helen uttered as James held an umbrella and escorted her through the wrought iron gate and up a rosebush lined flagstone path to the tiny door with small mullioned windows.

"May... they're here!" came a voice from inside the house.

Opening the door, a small gray-haired sprightly woman in a tunic randomly covered in dry paint reached for James and Helen and kissed them both warmly. "Welcome children! Lovely to meet you Helen, I'm Rose, dear."

"I've been so looking forward to meeting you."

Rose led them through a narrow hallway into a sitting room with low oak-beamed ceilings and a large bay window with a window seat facing the ocean. A thick rug covered most of the stone floor and against the far wall warmth emanated from a fireplace with blackened ornate ironwork and a simple over-mantle on which were a variety of family photos. In the center of the room was a heavy old mahogany coffee table and grouped around this were two armchairs and a comfortable old damask sofa. Two heavily ladened bookcases were built into alcoves on either side of the fireplace and the walls were densely covered with a variety of oil paintings.

Aunt May bustled into the room and kissed them both, saying, "Oh… you're here at last." In contrast to Rose she was a solid full-bosomed woman, her salt and pepper hair caught up loosely in a bun. "I was beginning to worry in this rain, James… Here, Helen, you sit here and warm yourself, I'll make a pot of tea. Do you like scones, dear?"

"Yes, I guess… well… actually, I've never tried one?"

"They're like biscuits," said James.

"No, they're not, James," corrected May.

"What we call biscuits they call cookies, and what we call scones they call biscuits."

May was completely confused but Rose seemed to understand, and added, "Well then, you're in for a real treat, because there is nothing in this world quite like the taste of fresh scones, Devonshire creme and strawberry jam… even if the scones are burnt."

The word burnt seemed to bring May out of her bewildered state, "Burnt, what's burnt?"

"Your scones will be unless you get them out of the oven!"

"Oh my!" said May on the run.

"James, we've made up grandfather's room for the two of you."

"Right… I'll get the things from the car."

"Well, my dear. I can see why our James is in love with you."

"Thank you."

"Is everything all right? James doesn't say, but something's wrong."

"Oh no, everything's fine. We just needed to get away." Seeing a canvas on an easel in the corner of the room, Helen pointed in its direction and asked, "Do you mind?"

"Not at all, but I'm no Constable." The scene depicted the view from the window looking out through the rain to the sloping garden that ended at a cluster of Monterey pines. Beyond that the visibility had been purposely blurred, blending the choppy gray sea into threatening low-lying clouds. "Beggars can't be choosers you see – if the weather's not obliging, I have to pick a window and make the most of it."

"It's very good. I love days like this – strange isn't it, but they seem to relax me more so than sunny days. Isn't that weird?"

"Not at all, dear. James is the same. When he came to stay with us as a little boy, my heart used to break watching him sit at this window looking out for hours at the rain. I think the dark clouds matched his feelings at that time... He was too young to deal with his father's death, and as much as May and I tried to compensate, we could never make up for the loss."

"But he talks about the two of you so affectionately. I know he loves both of you very much."

"I know he does, and that's nice of you to say, dear – but it's not really the same... is it?" Rose smiled warmly at Helen and it was not difficult to imagine how beautiful she must have been when she was younger.

"I suppose... I guess James told you about my mother. I was eight when she died."

"It leaves such an emptiness, but there's no reason you can't fill it full of happiness now. You'll always miss them, but if you have someone you love, and eventually have a family, you'll find you can get it all back again – you'll be in a different role this time, of course, but it can be done."

"You sound like my friend Maria. Without her, I don't know what would have become of me... I think I've sabotaged relationships to protect myself. I fear the future... I just hope James and I will be okay."

"You didn't sabotage them, dear – they weren't right to begin with, and I have a feeling you and James will be just fine... and the reason you worry about the future is because you're young. When I was young, I would spend a lot of my time thinking about the future, and now that I'm old I spend most of my time thinking about the past!"

"We do get on surprisingly well."

"Be yourself and always be honest with each other – most people see honesty as a weakness, when in fact it's a sign of strength. Only the confident are completely honest." Walking to the window. "Do you like the sea, my dear?"

"Yes, I live near the sea at home."

"Good. Then after tea, we shall put on our coats, and with our umbrellas at the ready, I shall show you our sea. It's quite wonderful, you know – always different, always the same."

Chapter 28

Rose and May sat at the dining room opposite Helen and James enjoying the satisfaction that followed a very good meal. A small fire burned in the old brick fireplace which had an oak beam mantle over which hung an antique mirror, and Rose continued her story. "...There were several young ladies who tagged along after James, and his friend... What was his name, James?"

Aunt May beat him to it. "Peter, wasn't it?"

"That's right, whatever happened to him? And there were NOT several girls that followed us."

Helen was enjoying James' embarrassment. "Now this I need to hear more about."

Reaching for the bottle James refreshed everyone's wine glass. "Were those your runner beans, Aunt May?

"Yes dear, a good crop this year."

Rose smiled. "You'll see Helen dear, how good he is at changing the subject."

"I noticed that."

"Now Helen, will you tell me what he's been up to?"

"Your very talented nephew has developed a system that lets you relive your past in explicit detail."

"Like a television?" Aunt May asked.

Helen continued, "No, you see it in your mind's eye. It's an odd experience... to revisit people and places from your past and see it all again – but in this case through adult eyes."

Rose asked. "You haven't reported this important

breakthrough, James?"

"No."

"And I can understand why. And what motivated you…" the penny dropped for Rose, "…Ah, John."

"Yes. I wanted to get to know him as an adult – I never expected it to work as well as it did."

"Seeing lost loved ones again – the desire would be quite potent."

After some thought, Rose asked, "Do you have it here?"

Rose was adamant, so James placed the headset on her and initialized the system while an anxious May sat beside her. James picked up the other headset. "This is a repeating headset – it lets me see whatever you're remembering."

Taking his arm. "If you don't mind, dear, I'll do this alone."

"Of course… Your thought controls the time period you access. Think of something quite recent to begin with… us having dinner, tonight, for instance."

"Don't fuss, James, I'll be fine."

James activated the system and Rose's view collapsed with a blink to nothingness. James, Helen and May watched as she tilted her head back slightly into a relaxed position, and then Rose experienced being pulled backwards through a corridor filled with revolving freeze-frames. Her apparent motion arrested before a large liquid-like three-dimensional image that moved slowly towards her, and then lunged forward, pulling her into the scene – the dining room, maybe twenty minutes earlier – 'This is incredible! My senses are alive!'

For a time she let her inner eye wander, focusing on details to get more accustomed with the system by going a little back and then forward from this time point – 'But, this is not where I want to be.'

Abruptly, she was pulled backwards at a much faster speed through countless frames for what seemed a long period, to another time and place. Here she saw a young man, circa 1940s, handing a much younger Rose a small ring, dropping to his knee in a joking gesture of convention.

James, Helen and May hear the shocked inward breath from Rose, and then, "Gerald!"

Aunt May nods. "I thought so. Two days after they were married he was deployed. They never saw each other again – he died on the beach at Normandy."

Rose flitted through a series of memories – a happy wedding, joyful reception with friends and family with many of the men and women in uniform. A final scene showed Rose and Gerald kissing passionately as he hung out the window of a train, and as the train left his waves were lost in the engines billowing smoke.

Rose was now sobbing and the three of them looked on anxiously as she said, "Oh Gerald... I have missed you so."

Rose brought herself back to the present, the system disengaged, and tears were running down her cheeks.

James took her in his arms. "I'm so sorry... I'm so very sorry."

Pulling away and smiling through tears, she kissed him. "No, James, that was the greatest gift anyone could ever give me."

Chapter 29

As Helen stood amongst the gorse and purple heather petting the wild Dartmoor ponies, James leaned against the car and finished a sandwich Aunt May had included in a well-stocked picnic basket. Looking out across the barren expanse of moorland, lonely farmhouses, and steep tumbled fields enclosed by lichen-covered stonewalls he was overcome by a feeling of almost unbearable nostalgia.

It felt strange to be going back to the same hotel and the same small village after more than twenty years. Every year, for as far back as he could remember, his family stayed at the Polurrian Hotel in Mullion for their summer vacation. His father had always traveled the same route through Devon and Cornwall, stopping off at the same spots to break up the drive. "You'll be going to Mullion again this year," neighbors would ask, and in response his father would reply without hesitation, "Oh yes, same as usual."

It seemed that every family had their own 'fortnight holiday spot' and there was almost an invisible force that drew them back year after year. 'Maybe that was the attraction,' he thought – the feeling of security and comfort that comes from following a familiar pattern.

The drive took all day, and it was early evening when they entered Mullion. Driving around the narrow road that circled the fifteenth century granite church, James was relieved and amazed to see that nothing had changed – in fact, the old village appeared to have been perfectly preserved.

"There's the Old Inn, the post office, and that small cottage that looks like someone's home... is the bank. I can't believe it – it hasn't changed a bit."

A few minutes outside the town, towards Mullion cove, was the hotel. Set in acres of landscaped gardens, the white Edwardian building with high bay windows facing the sea sat on top of three hundred-foot cliffs. Walking into the reception area, James carefully scrutinized the interior and was again delighted to see that, other than a few minor alterations, the hotel had still maintained its atmosphere of comfort and elegance.

Receiving a message from Pete at reception, he called when they were shown to their room.

"Pete, it's James – I got your message."

"Oh, hi, James."

"Is everything okay?"

"Yeah, I just wanted to find out if you found Colin Hawthorne?"

"We're going there today. Cadgewith is a ten-minute drive from here. I'll call you the moment I have news."

"How was it with your family?"

"Great. We had a wonderful time. You know we've only been away a few days and yet it feels like weeks... Are you sure everything's okay?"

"I'm fine, just some strange things going on at work... I don't know. My captain is all over me – never gave a damn before... Oh yeah, and before I forget, does Helen know a man named Karl List?"

James asked Helen and held the phone so Pete could hear her response. "He's Erik's Political Advisor and confidante, but he seems to do more than that. He and Erik have worked together

147

for as long as I can remember. He never comes into the house –
he lives at Erik's ranch."

"Did you hear that, Pete?"

"Yes. That's about all I know about him too. My father had
a picture of him in his file… Anyhow, I'll let you go, and have a
good time."

"Thanks, Pete, I'll call when I have some news."

***

There was no room for cars in the small Cornish fishing village
of Cadgewith so they parked on the outskirts and walked down
the steep streets bordered by immaculately maintained thatched
cottages. Small stone huts clung perilously to the rocky cliffs
either side of a pebbly beach laden with beached fishing boats. A
row of small shops and a tearoom lined the center of the village.
The door to the newsagent was open and a man who looked like
the proprietor sat on a bench just outside the door reading a
newspaper.

"Good morning, I'm trying to find Porth Cottage," asked
James.

In a broad Cornish accent, "You'd be looking for Colin
Hawthorne?"

"That's right."

"Well, I can save you the walk – 'e's right there, working on
'is boat." Pointing to the other side of the pebbly beach. "The old
gent in the wellies and woolly jumper."

"Thanks very much."

Calling after them, "He bought that little sailing boat when
he retired. Spends all day, every day, working on it – never takes
it out, mind."

Trudging across the stony beach and weaving their way around a variety of fishing boats and equipment they reached an older man with a weather-beaten face giving a coat of paint to an already pristine craft. "Good morning... Mr. Hawthorne?" questioned James.

"Yes," he responded gruffly not lifting his eyes from his work.

"My name is James Moore and this is Helen Thompson."

"I'd come straight to the point if I were you – I'm busy."

"We have come from California to talk to you about..."

Still continuing with his paintbrush stroke. "You'd be something to do with that American chap who keeps calling. Well, I didn't want to talk to him, and I don't want to talk to you."

James paused momentarily. "The reason we came in person is because we think you may be able to help us, you see..."

"I suggest you leave young man, while I'm still able to maintain a civil tongue."

James turned towards Helen and raised his eyebrows, and she nodded signaling that she would try.

"My name is Helen, sir, and we really do need your help."

At the sound of her voice a scrawny black and white cat emerged from the cabin and bounded up to her. This seemed to get Colin Hawthorne's attention and he stopped painting and looked at Helen questioningly.

"You're a friendly little kitty, what's your name?" she said bending to stroke the cat as it entwined itself around her legs.

"His name's Tigger, and he's not normally sociable with strangers."

Relieved Helen had broken the ice, James added, "And he stays with you while you work?"

His question went unanswered, but not out of rudeness,

Colin was watching this exchange closely. Placing the brush carefully on top of the can of paint, he wiped his hands on an old rag and climbed down. "What did you say your name was, young lady?"

"Helen... Helen Thompson."

"Old Tigger seems quite taken with you."

As James watched him chatting with Helen, he could see Colin's cold exterior melting away to reveal a lonely man with a gentle nature. They talked for nearly an hour sitting on a large washed-up piece of timber. Colin listened carefully as Helen explained the reason for their visit, and resting her hand gently on his arm, added, "...We didn't want to upset you. I hope you know that."

Embarrassed to find his eyes filling with unaccustomed tears, Colin turned his head away. "Please forgive me, both of you, I'm sorry for my rudeness, young man... We were very happy you see, and you remind me so much of Helga."

"You don't have any other family?"

"No. We never had children, my brother died ten years back, so I'm all alone now... That's why I get her ready you see," he said pointing to his boat. "I'm going to sail off one day into a bad storm and not come back, the trouble is... I don't have the courage."

"You mustn't think that way, and in an indirect way we're related since your wife's son, Erik, is my adopted uncle."

Colin looked baffled at this statement, and after a delay James decided to make a suggestion. "There's a tea room just near the bakery. Would you like to join us for tea or coffee?"

"No, no, no, no, I've been very rude. Come back to my cottage and I'll make a pot of tea."

Chapter 30

The night was ominously dark, and the thick black clouds all but obliterated whatever light was shed from the slither of a moon. A shadow wiped past the Jacuzzi and the toys strewn across the deck and lawn. The neighborhood was silent except for the occasional distant echoing bark of a restless dog.

A second shadow entered the yard but in this instance they could be identified as an operative dressed in black fatigues. There were two, and as one scanned the area using a night vision eyepiece the other picked the lock on a side door leading into the garage. Using an earpiece communicator, "Please verify alarm system is disabled?"

Glancing at an instrument on his belt: "Alarm disabled."

Inside, they quietly carried out their assigned tasks with military precision.

Whispering, "Telemetry?"

"On, and... operational, sir."

"Good to go?"

"Yes, sir."

Locking the garage door, they leapt over the back fence, jogged into the canyon and climbed up to a ridge overlooking the peaceful suburb. While she prepared two concealed off-road dirt bikes from behind a set of large boulders, he studied the displayed readings.

"Reading is rising – I estimate fifteen minutes."

Adrenaline was still high, and they both pulled their

handguns in a split-second draw when a coyote ran past carrying a jackrabbit in its mouth. Returning their guns to their holsters, they waited impatiently, switching their attention between the house and the rapidly rising reading on their monitoring device.

"Threshold reached, activate player."

Sheryl rolled over and shook Paul, who was in a deep sleep. "Scott's left the TV on."

"Umm, what?"

"It sounds like cartoons."

"Okay. Go back to sleep, I'll check," said Paul, reluctantly dragging himself out of bed.

On the crest, the female operative pointed in the direction of the house. "Upstairs light, sir."

Scott was out like a light, and the television off. Still groggy, Paul turned his head from side-to-side trying to decipher where the music was coming from, finally deciding it was the garage. At the security panel he stopped. "I must have forgot." The moment he opened the garage door, an overpowering smell of gas enveloped him and as he reached for the light switch, he lifted his sleeve to his mouth. While fumbling for the switch, he stared in bewilderment at the unfamiliar tape player on the floor as it blared out a nursery rhyme.

As all the lights went on, except for one, Paul stared in fascinated horror as he saw the two exposed contacts within a cracked-open glass light bulb, spark and ignite the gas. A ball of fire incinerated him and swept almost instantly throughout the house engulfing it in flames.

The two operatives on the high ridge witnessed the windows of the house punched out by the force of the powerful explosion and saw the neighborhood temporarily lit up like daylight by the explosion. The female operative searched the burning structure with binoculars.

"Anyone?"

"No, sir."

"Okay, that's long enough for a confirmed kill. Let's go."

With the dirt bike engines off initially and using their brakes sparingly, they rode expertly down the opposite side of the hill, and when they reached the street, started the engines to drive them into a waiting van, with a ramp extended. Once in, the ramp was retracted, the doors closed and the van departed.

When they had settled themselves in their seats, Karl in a front seat, swiveled around to face them.

"Report."

"Mission accomplished, sir."

"Confirm details."

"We used fuse wire to bypass the water heater's thermocouple and a standard light bulb as an igniter. The child's player had been modified for remote activation and to monitor gas level. All will be destroyed by the fire and an investigator will report the incident as accidental."

"Good, that is most satisfactory."

Chapter 31

Like its owner, Porth Cottage had suffered from neglect. A thick green moss almost completely covered the slate roof, the front and back garden were heavily overgrown, and the thick stonewalls needed to be patched and painted. Two open windows brought a breath of fresh air into the small living room that held a faint smell of stale tobacco smoke. A black ironwork fireplace held the ashen remnants of a fire and on the wooden mantelpiece stood the only framed picture in the room.

James peered closely at the photo. "You do bear a resemblance to Helga."

"Hmm, I suppose so."

Glancing around the room James noticed the brass nautical accents on the walls and the high decorative ledge circling the room that had a lifetime of mementos coated with a thick layer of dust. A collection of pipes, half-used packets of tobacco, matches and an ashtray lay neatly on a small table next to an armchair that faced an old television set – the only evidence of comfort in an otherwise solitary existence.

The sound of cupboard doors and the clatter of silverware came from the kitchen. "I only have digestive biscuits to have with our tea."

"They're my favorite," James answered.

"Are you sure you don't want me to give you a hand?" Helen asked.

"No, no, no, no. Make yourself at home, I'll only be a tick."

The living room extended into a small dining room with a table and four chairs, sideboard, and French doors leading into the long but narrow back garden. James and Helen seated themselves at the dining room table as several stacks of old books and newspapers crowded the threadbare sofa.

"Ah, that's a good idea," Colin said, entering the room and setting the tray on the table. It was laden with a variety of old mugs - stained and chipped, a brown teapot, bowl of sugar, plate of biscuits, and a polished sterling silver milk jug which he had fished out in honor of the occasion. "Sorry about the mugs – I'm not used to company you see."

Tigger leapt onto Colin's lap and settled himself after a lot of circling, purring and kneading. Stroking his rough fur, Colin collected his thoughts and began to recount his version of the facts. "She was the daughter of Günther Kluge, a highly decorated U-boat commander killed in action a few months before we met. Her papers listed her residence as Ordensburg, the Fuehrer's Nazi college in Vogelsang. She spoke perfect English, and in the year that followed we became lovers, married, and I brought her here when my tour was up."

"So you didn't help her look for her child?" asked Helen.

"No, no, no... She told me nothing of that until years later... At first, I wasn't sure if she loved me or just wanted to get out of Germany... but I loved her, and I know she came to love me."

"What did you know at that time?" asked James.

"Helga was sent to Ordensburg when she was ten – it was a sort of elite seminary of arrogance, racial prejudice, and the techniques of tyranny. A nursery for perpetuating the Nazi philosophy, and this was what they wanted to do, replace reason and tolerance with hatred and force... The memories from those days kept coming back to her. She'd wake at night sometimes in

155

a cold sweat and try to throttle me."

"Did she ever go for any counseling?" asked Helen.

"Nay, none of us did – we just got on with it. I read somewhere about how young people have to go off and find themselves… huh, in those days, we didn't even know we were lost!"

James and Helen both smiled. "What about this college?"

"She told me everything in the end…"

A group of uniformed fourteen-year old Hitler youth stood on the hockey field with Ordensburg College in the background. An instructor demonstrated the correct operation of the Luger handgun and finished by firing a shot into a distant haystack.

He then called out the name, Kurt Dietl, and a strapping young man walked forward and repeated the procedure flawlessly. A transport truck entered the picture and the young Helga was wringing her hands behind her back nervously.

"Ordensburg was the flagship of five. They had classes on everything from espionage to selective breeding, to drawing-room etiquette and horsemanship. She wept one night hysterically, and told me how the academy's officers had each of them kill a prisoner from the local concentration camp. This way, they could get them past the disabling trauma of first kill before they were loaned out for battlefield experience."

An emaciated older woman in threadbare rags was dragged from the truck by a soldier and led over to the young Kurt. The young boy circled the woman slowly, lifted her lowered head to look her in the eyes, raised the gun to her forehead, turned to his instructor, who nodded, and he pulled the trigger. The young Helga's eyes blinked and she shuddered.

James and Helen faces showed stunned abhorrence.

"She was a top student and great athlete, which is why she

was chosen for the master race program – It was a great honor – they mated the best with the best - and that's where the child came from – you said his name's Erik?"

"Yes."

"When the war went bad for them, they took the boy from her and put him in the care of a guardian who was supposed to get the child to South America."

"Who was this guardian?"

"He was at Ordensburg with Helga. She said he was strong and smart – but ruthless. Kurt Dietl was his name... it's all in the satchel."

James looked up quickly. "Satchel?"

"Bit naughty of me that – I was supposed to confiscate everything but I had a bit of a soft spot for Helga right from the start – I kept it for her until she was released."

"Do you still have this satchel?"

Colin turned in his chair, removed an old leather satchel from the sideboard and emptied the contents onto the table. There was a silver locket containing a picture of Helga's parents, some old coins, and a small leather writing case. Colin unclipped the writing case's clasp and pushed it towards them. In it were a few old photographs and a diary.

As they looked through the items, Colin picked up a worn photograph of Helga at around nine, beaming a smile on the deck of a passenger ship as her parents gazed down at her lovingly.

"Her mother died of influenza soon after this trip – she said this was her last happy memory as a child."

James studied an Ordensburg class photo and the ancient shield in the center of the group on which he could just make out the word 'Fahnenbrueder'. "Hmm, Fahnenbrueder... Brotherhood of the flag?"

"Is that what it means? Helga would say it in her nightmares."

"Do you mind?" James asked pointing to Helga's diary.

"Go ahead, son – can you speak German?"

"A little."

"Take all of this with you, for all I care."

" No, we couldn't," Helen said.

"They were dark days – I don't want to be reminded of them."

"I could make copies and bring it back?" James suggested.

"No. Good riddance to bad rubbish – I hope it helps you."

Colin picked up another picture of Helga. "The police found her body washed up on the shore near Penzance. They said she must have fallen – but she didn't… They even thought I'd killed her for a while – insult on injury that was."

"I'm sorry," Helen said trying to comfort him.

"It's all over and done with now, m' dear."

Helen picked up a few of the coins and jingled them. "We know a little boy who will be thrilled to add these to his collection… thank you, you've been very kind to us."

"Nonsense, it's been good to have some company… y' know people say your memory fades as you get older, but it's not true, mine's clearer than ever. I don't think about the future anymore, and the present puts very few demands on me, and so my mind's turned its full attention on the past – it's a torture really… Oh well, no use feeling sorry for myself. I've enjoyed meeting you both."

As James and Helen walked down the path, Colin waved a final farewell. The reminiscences of the afternoon had churned up the past, and Colin had a clear memory of Helga walking down to the small pebbly cove between the rugged cliffs. On seeing his wife from his fishing boat Colin greeted her with a kiss, and she passed him a packed meal and thermos of strong tea, he teased her about something and she waved him off dismissively with a smile. Ready to go, he signaled to the driver of a tractor who gave the boat a shove to roll it down on a bed of round logs out into the water, at which time the engine was engaged, they turned, and went out to sea.

Chapter 32

Lying recumbent on his bed and hearing the clock chime the hour Pete could feel his temper simmering. It was now two a.m., and each failed attempt to sleep left him progressively more frustrated and irritable. Try as he might he could find neither rhyme nor reason for the recent change in attitude towards him from supervisors. Without all of the facts at his disposal, however, this attempt to second-guessing their motive was predestined for failure.

"This is crazy… it would be less tiring not to try at all."

Launching himself off the bed he grabbed a beer from the refrigerator and went through to the living room. Piles of papers were strewn throughout the room in some semblance of order, so he had to weave his way through this labyrinth in order to reach the center of the room.

Grabbing the remote he turned on the television and threw himself into the nearest armchair. Pete had always found it difficult to relax. His abundant energy and dynamic personality meant he tended to push himself to the limit making it extremely difficult for him to unwind at the end of the day – his body ran on a fuel of anxiety. Fidgeting and restless he couldn't even concentrate on the corny love story currently being aired so he flicked through the channels and finally settled on the news.

The anchor continued, "… a twenty to thirty cent increase in the price per gallon at the pump is expected… In local news, Mayor Erik Banner's special police unit TASK, successfully ended an extensive undercover operation today with the arrest of fourteen suspects and the seizure of 6 tons of narcotics in a tunnel running under the border. Mayor Banner, who personally financed TASK had this to say."

Erik Banner stood outside city council offices being interviewed, with the city and state flags as a backdrop. "I'm elated and very proud of the men and women of TASK."

The reporter asked, "Would you say your investment has paid off?"

"I have never counted the cost of this in dollars and cents…"

Pete added. "Yeah, right."

"…But I did lay down a challenge for the TASK unit – and today they came through with flying colors."

The scene cut back to the TV studio where a wider shot showed a male and female anchor, who had monitored the interview, and now would add comment.

"Well done TASK, and a big thank you to our mayor."

"If he can do this much on a local level, imagine how effective he could be statewide."

Pete grabbed the remote and almost broke it in half when he pressed the 'power' button to turn off the TV. "Don't say that, that's just what he wants you…"

He had spoken to James over an hour ago and knew it would be at least a few more hours before he called back with any news. He gazed morosely around the room making spluttering noises with his lips.

Smoking always seemed to relax him and over the years he had discovered a leisurely stroll round the block and a cigarette would often do the trick. He picked up a packet from the coffee table and rummaged feverishly through it only to discover it was empty, as was the carton in the kitchen. "Damn!" he shouted, screwing up the carton and chucking it across the room.

Muttering irritably to himself he pulled on some clothes, grabbed his keys, wallet and cell-phone, and left through the back door, heading to the local all-night convenience store. This was reached more easily by cutting through the alleyway at the end of his backyard, and as he walked down the path and out through the back gate he took in lungful's of the cool night air, gradually feeling his tension subside. The peace and quiet was restful and the distant hum of occasional passing cars seemed to further soothe his frayed nerves.

Emerging from the alley he turned to check for traffic, and seeing the path was clear, crossed to the other side. Pete's family home was in the small town of La Mesa. His parents had bought it in the 1950s, and after his mother's death a year ago he decided to move back. The most striking feature about all the homes in this area was their reduced size. Everything from the front porches, shuttered windows and single garages, to their well-tended lawns and flower gardens were almost two-thirds that of today's, giving the neighborhood its own distinctive charm. Very few cars were ever parked on the street as most of Pete's neighbors were elderly, and even if they still drove, their cars were usually garaged overnight.

This unusual scaled size made the large four-door sedan stand out like a sore thumb, especially when an occupant opened their door to pour the remains of his drink into the gutter and the cab light flashed on momentarily. The scene had all the trademarks of a covert police surveillance operation, and Pete would have thought nothing more of it, if it weren't for the fact they were parked in a perfect position to observe his house.

"Ridiculous… there's no reason," he mumbled, shaking his head to clear the fogginess from his brain. Believing that a lack of sleep must have let his mind slip from precaution to paranoia, he continued on his way convinced that by the time he returned they would more than likely be gone. After all, in situations like this, officers had always been told to ignore any undercover operation so as not to compromise the safety and cover of the personnel involved. Although circumstances at work recently had made him extremely suspicious, he could see no reason why this would have anything to do with him.

Despite it being three a.m., the store was bright and welcoming. "Evening Pete – what's up?" said the large hearty storeowner, clutching a can of coke and turning away from the television.

"Nothing much. How are you, Josh?"

"Well, thanks... Cigarettes?"

"Thanks." He paid quickly and headed back home. He hoped the vehicle would have left by now, but his hopes were dashed when he rounded the corner and found the situation unchanged. Deciding to observe the observers, he took cover between a tree and a high fence, knelt down and telephoned the dispatcher at police headquarters. Giving his detective ID number along with the license plate number of the car, he asked for its present location. The dispatcher confirmed that the car was on police business, however, it was supposed to be on an assignment in Del Mar.

Pete sat down, crossed his legs and decided to wait it out. An hour and a quarter passed with no change. Eventually, his uncomfortable position made his muscles feel restricted and cramped, so after stretching his limbs in all directions he repositioned himself with his head resting between the slats of the fence. Now more comfortable, he made a vain attempt to stay awake, but exhaustion had finally caught up with him, and the peaceful darkness together with the gentle soughing of the trees lulled him into a deep sleep.

Asleep and snoring, Pete completely missed the arrival of a large black van with opaquely tinted windows concealing whoever was within. Switching off their headlights and engine the moment it turned the corner it glided silently into position directly behind the police car. It was the loud clunk of the closing car doors reverberating through the silence of the night that jerked him out of his slumber.

Pete was immediately wide-awake and watched as two officers approached the passenger window of the van, recognizing them as his unit Lieutenant and department Captain – the same two men who had been making his work life so stressful lately. Unable to hear the content of the conversation they were having with the person in the van, he had to be satisfied with what he could visually conclude from the exchange. Their posture and gestures were deferential telling him they seemed to be reporting to someone in higher authority, and shortly after, they returned to their car and drove off.

The van sat there ominously, and just as Pete was beginning to believe that they were simply a shift relief, the rear door opened and four men, armed and dressed like a SWAT unit jumped out and ran towards his house. Two ran to the back and out of sight while the other two crouched either side of the front door working on the lock. They had it open in seconds, nodded to each other, and fired a spread of bullets into the house, the sound muted by their silencers.

Covering each other like an expertly choreographed routine they entered the house and from that moment on Pete could only hear the faint sound of muffled short sub machine gun bursts and flashes of light. His eyes blinked and his body flinched with every burst of bullets. Their chosen method for searching the house was to lay down a barrage into each new area, leaving no doubt in his mind their objective was not to apprehend, but to execute.

Dragging himself to his feet he backed away slowly at first, lost his footing as he stumbled over a tree root, and then turned and ran off in frantic flight.

Chapter 33

A primeval fear consumed him, temporarily incapacitating his ability to think logically. Not knowing where to go, he fled blindly down the still-darkened streets towards the nearest bright lights, eventually finding himself at the nearby trolley station. Clambering aboard the waiting streetcar he collapsed, panting into the nearest seat, just before the doors closed and it pulled away. Oblivious to the stares from the few people aboard, he sat motionless while he caught his breath, gazing out of the window as the trolley rocked and rolled down the tracks.

After a few moments he leaned forward, cupped his head in his hands, and pressing his fingers into his eye sockets muttering, "Assholes sold me out."

Lifting his head he looked at his hands that shook uncontrollably. As a homicide detective he had been exposed to many gruesome acts of violence over the years, and had in time developed a sort of thick skin that insulated him from their effects. The difference in this instance, however, was that this was personal. He recognized his shocked state – he had seen it before on the faces of victims who had narrowly escaped death. Only now, he regretted his lack of compassion and indifference he had shown to their predicament.

Sitting up, he leaned back, reached into his pocket and pulled out his keys. Flicking through them he selected one with a green tag, on which the following words were written, 'Thanks Pete, see you in a few months, Jim.'

Jim Westford, Pete's partner and friend, had taken a three-month leave of absence in order to accept a well-paid training contract in Kazakhstan. The former Russian republic was trying to establish a professional police force to combat the rapidly escalating crime rate that had soared after communist control had loosened its iron grip. Although there was nothing that needed to be done on a regular basis, Jim had asked Pete if he would periodically check on the house whenever he was in the neighborhood. When the trolley pulled into the nearby station, he jogged to Jim's house and let himself in. Heading straight for the phone, he pulled his wallet out of his back pocket, removed a list of phone numbers that James had given him before he left, dialed the number for the hotel in Cornwall, and asked for James Moore.

"I'll try his room, sir."

Pete drummed his fingers on the nearby table with increasing force.

"I'm afraid there's no answer from his room, would you like to leave a message?" The impersonal tone of the English operator irritated his already frayed nerves.

"Well, could you try paging him – I'm calling from California and this is an emergency."

"Of course, sir, please hold the line."

After a long pause the operator returned, "I'm sorry, sir, but he can't be found. If you would like to leave your name and number, I'll have the receptionist give him the message the moment he returns."

"Hmm… Okay. Could you tell him that Pete Hammond telephoned and that it is very urgent he calls me. Tell him not to call me at home and don't bother trying my cell phone I turned it off and if I don't hear anything I'll try calling back in about thirty minutes – did you get that?"

After confirming the message, and assuring him they would deliver it to James, Pete hung up the phone. For a moment or two he stood there, relieved that the feeling of panic had subsided, and that he was beginning to think clearly again. With a profound sigh he placed his hands on the telephone table and leaned heavily on them taking deep breaths. It seemed that at least for a while he was safe.

As his pulse slowed and the shock subsided, he became acutely aware he was hungry and so rummaged through the kitchen. Jim had cleared out all of the perishables before he left, and so after scavenging through the starkly stocked larder and refrigerator, he could only come up with a jar of instant coffee, a can of chili, and a box of dry crackers – not the most appetizing early morning breakfast, but then needs must. He took this dubious meal on a tray through to the living room and sat down to eat, gazing around at the unfamiliar surroundings. Typical of a bachelor's pad, Jim had equipped the house with all of the basic necessities, but no real comfort. A sofa, two mismatched chairs, and a coffee table were all arranged to face a large-screen television, and against the wall leading to the bedroom Pete could see Jim's gun cabinet.

Hurriedly finishing his meal he made a beeline for the display case, forced the lock, and took a nine-millimeter handgun with four loaded clips, and a pump-action shotgun with a box of shells. "Now come and get me, you assholes," he said, spitting out the words venomously. Heading into the bedroom, he scoured the contents of drawers and the closet until he found a large baggy jacket and a baseball cap, which being two sizes too large, were ideal to heavily disguise his appearance.

"Where are they?" he grumbled. Studying the sheet of paper James had given him, he noticed a handwritten note at the bottom of the page, which read, "If there are any unforeseen problems contact my friend Paul Barnes," and he had listed an address and phone number."

He glanced at his watch. It was around five a.m. – a little early to be making telephone calls, but then necessity overruled etiquette in this instance. He dialed Paul's home number and leaned against the wall as he waited for the ringing tone. Surprised to hear neither a ring nor a busy tone he assumed he had misdialed, and so he hung up and carefully tried the number again.

"That's odd…" he mumbled after receiving the same strange response and so he called the operator.

"I don't know, sir. I've checked the line and I can only tell you there must be a fault somewhere. I'll put in a work order and get a technician to go out and isolate the problem."

"Okay… thanks." Puzzled, he stood for a moment, tapping the phone against his chin thoughtfully. A wave of trepidation swept over him.

Slamming down the receiver, he grabbed his things and Jim's car keys, and left for Paul's house.

***

"Let's go straight into lunch Helen, I'm famished," said James as they strolled into the lobby of the hotel. After leaving Colin Hawthorne, they had meandered through the tiny village of Cadgewith admiring the picturesque thatched cottages and enjoying the mild spring day.

"That's a great idea, I'm…"

"Excuse me, Mr. Moore," interrupted a young woman at reception, "There's an urgent message for you from a Mr. Pete

Hammond. He wanted you to contact him at once – I have a phone number where he can be reached."

"That's okay, I have his number."

"But Mr. Moore, he was quite adamant you only call him at the number given, and said that you should not call him on his mobile since he has it turned off."

Looking at each other with foreboding, they took the communication, returned promptly to their suite and James tried the number given to no avail. "There is nothing worse than receiving an urgent message to call someone, and then not getting an answer."

"What could have happened? Pete told them that it was an emergency."

He compared the number on the message against the list Pete had given him, "You know, Helen, this number doesn't match any Pete gave me."

"Do you think the receptionist wrote it down wrong?"

"I don't think so. They got the area code right… but the last seven digits are not even close to anything I have for him."

"I'm going to make a coffee. Would you like one, James?" Helen asked as she turned on the electric kettle and poured a packet of coffee grounds into a press pot.

"That'll be nice," he answered distractedly, staring at the piece of paper.

"What's the time in California?"

Glancing at the bedside alarm clock, he quickly subtracted eight hours from the time displayed. "Just after six in the morning."

"Then why don't you try calling him at home – he probably hasn't left for work yet."

James hesitated for only a moment while he read again the

explicit instructions on the message, and then dialed Pete's home number. The phone rang several times, and just as he was about to abandon the attempt, it was picked up. "Pete? Thank heavens I got you. What's going on?"

An eerie silence pervaded, and as the pause lengthened, James could sense an uneasy feeling mounting in him. This was heightened by the faint but sinister sound of somebody breathing. Just as he was about to hang up, a man with a gravel-like voice said, "This is Sergeant Bill Wallace of the San Diego Police. Maybe you can help me, sir, do you know where we can find Pete Hammond... He didn't show up for work and, well frankly, we're a bit worried about him." There was a troubling inconsistency between these words of concern and the lack of emotion in which they were conveyed that alerted James. However, intent on using this opportunity, he tried to sound as obliging as possible in hopes that it would lull his party into a false sense of security.

"Well of course, officer, now let me see. I have a number written down here somewhere. You see, I received an urgent message from him asking me to call him right back... Let me see now, it's here somewhere..."

"Thank you for your help. Any information you can give us will be much appreciated, sir. I'm sorry to have to trouble you with this."

"Oh, it's no trouble at all. I'm only too happy to help."

"Well, that's a nice attitude, Mr. Moore."

"Ah..." James said abruptly changing his tone, "I don't know who you are, but I never told you my name," and with that he put the phone down.

"I don't like the sound of this at all Helen, we must get in touch with Pete and find out what the hell is going on."

Still getting no answer from the number Pete had given he

tried Paul's home number with no success, further compounding his confusion and concern.

"You know there's something not quite right here," he said, reiterating the content of the calls.

"I think we should get back, James. Don't you?"

"Yes, I'm afraid I do."

Pulling out a suitcase from the closet and beginning to pack, Helen smiled reassuringly, "Don't worry, we've got the satchel now, and I'm sure it should clear all of this up."

"You're right, let's get going as quick as we can. We'll have room service pack us a lunch and we'll eat on the way. I'll call the airlines, it will be quicker if we drive to Exeter, drop off the car, and then catch a commuter flight to London... I'll leave a message with the receptionist telling Pete that we're on our way back, along with the new flight details."

***

Dawn had just started to lighten the cloudy morning, and it was hard to tell whether the grayness came from the early morning mist, or the murky smoke-laden air. A police barricade blocked the entrance to the street listed on James' note, so Pete parked the car and walked the remainder of the way. An acrid stench of fumes prevailed and falling ash showered the neighborhood like a snow flurry. Turning the corner, the charred remains of a house came into view, lit up by fire truck searchlights and a few remaining flames from the scorched framework. A crowd of people encircled the cordoned off area dressed in robes, having been abruptly awakened from their sleep. Pete carefully studied the house number printed on the curb in front of the burned-out remnants and compared it with the note from James – the numbers matched. Walking up to a fire inspector he flipped open his wallet to show his identification. "What happened?"

Wiping the sweat from his blackened brow, he took a seat on the in-step of a fire truck. "It looks like gas leaked out of the water heater overnight and somehow ignited. Poor people... they never stood a chance."

"No one escaped?"

"No... Husband, wife and a boy. All killed... I've never seen one go up like this before."

Chapter 34

Their last-minute rescheduled return trip left them very little time between connections in London and Dallas, so they were personally hurried through customs and immigration by the airline. "I don't know Helen, this is all a little hectic," James said as they boarded the plane for the final eight-hour leg of the journey home, "but all in all I think I prefer a high-speed dash between gates rather than lengthy layovers."

Making their way quickly down the aisle, they were relieved to see the plane was half empty and they had a whole row of seats to themselves. They stowed their larger bags in the overhead bin and collapsed into their seats. Helen pushed her seat back and rested her head. "If you don't mind, James, I think I'll take a little nap, I feel exhausted."

"Go ahead, love, I feel tired too but there's something I've got to do first."

When the plane had taken off and leveled, the captain sanctioned the use of electronic equipment, so James pulled out his laptop and positioned it on the pull-down table in front of him.

Helen woke to find James reading Helga's diary. "Found anything new?"

James could now give a detailed history from this personal account.

A sixteen-year-old Helga in a swimsuit and goggles stood ready on the starting block of an Olympic size pool, alongside another young woman who could pass as her twin. The gun sounded and they both lunged forward, surface diving, breaking quickly into a rapid free-style stroke.

"The diary begins when she arrived in Berlin, at the start of a rigorous personal evaluation program that occupied her from morning to night for a fortnight. She had to compete against her instructor, while a group of silent observers looked on. These tests checked her physical fitness, education, and intelligence – in most cases Helga, and this Miss Eva, were equally matched."

Helga was at an elegant dinner party in which she finished playing a piano piece by Wagner, was appreciatively applauded by what looked to be the best of society, and was hugged and kissed proudly by Miss Eva.

"After countless medical examinations, she was questioned on her political, social and religious beliefs, and her family line was checked, for what she called, impurities. In the evenings, she was taken to the opera, theater, and dinner parties to determine her breeding and class. Passing the ordeal with high grades, she underwent the artificial insemination procedure on February 4th, 1944, talking constantly of the supreme honor at having been chosen. Throughout the pregnancy Miss Eva visited – most pleased with her progress."

A screaming Helga on a stainless-steel operating table surrounded by doctors during labor. The delivery room was dark, except for one bright overhead lamp. In a break in contractions she reached out, pleading with someone off in the distance, and Miss Eva stood with several men in military uniforms looking on.

"The relationship soured a few weeks before the birth after Helga requested to be involved with the child's upbringing. In later entries, her attitude had rapidly deteriorated, and a Kurt Dietl had arrived to act as the child's guardian, with her involvement limited to only feeding."

Helga woke in an unknown hotel room, having been drugged she leapt to her feet, disoriented. Twisting around frantically she opened a cupboard and drawers to find her clothes, and then stared with dread at a suitcase on the bed. Flipping open the lid, her knees buckled, and she sobbed, crying, "Nein, nein, nein." Now, almost hysterical, she grabbed the handle of the case and threw it aside creating a shower of money that filled the room.

Helen lift's the diary. "That poor woman."

"It's tragic... that's strange," holding the in-flight phone, "I can't pick up messages... Butler it's me, any messages?"

The Butler replied, "Complete voice verification required."

"Huh, Butler, the quick brown fox jumped over the lazy dog."

"Please hold the line... Good afternoon, sir, how can I help you?"

"Butler, why did you initiate a lockout?"

"There have been five illegal attempts to gain computer access, sir."

"Butler, what is your security status?"

"Security is operational and armed – all sensors are inactive, data access has been disabled, sir."

"What's going on, James?"

"Somebody tried to hack into my home system – probably nothing. Butler, playback messages." James relayed a message as he listened, "Paul called – Two police officers came to the University with a warrant to search our records for a student... he set Arthur on them."

"Who's Arthur?"

"He's a robot – very sophisticated. Paul and I have been working on him for years. My guess is that Paul was so irritated, that he went to a lab and used a terminal to turn on Arthur – his home base is in my office. He probably told him to run the 'stealth seek and record program', and limited it to our office area – we sometimes have Arthur sneak around the corridors catching students that are late for class. He would have followed the men at a discreet distance and recorded everything they say and do."

Chortling, she asked, "What does Arthur look like?"

"Oh, he's short and shaped like a cube. He only has one arm, but he's very versatile. He would have recorded everything on a CD in his optical drive."

Helen seemed fascinated with this robot and wanted to know more. "Where did you get the name Arthur from?"

"That's a bit of a silly story."

"Well, tell me anyway."

"There was a friend I knew years ago. He was a little strange…"

"Unfriendly strange?"

"No, not at all. He was a real salt of the earth type, and, well, let's just say that he marched to the beat of a different drummer. He never went to college, and yet almost every time we got together, I would end up looking stupid. He never said it directly, but I know he thought I was just wasting my time at university. His logic was just… different. Anyway, one summer break, he and his wife invited me over for dinner. When I arrived, I noticed he had a cat and a dog, and so naturally I asked what their names were. As he was handing me a drink he said, 'Ceifa and Deifa'. Well, I of course assumed that the origin was either Greek or Latin… and so I asked him, and then it happened again."

"What?"

"Well, he just stopped what he was doing and gave me a sort of puzzled look, that seemed to doubt whether I had any common sense at all, and said, 'It's just C-fer cat, and D-fer dog.'"

Helen chuckled as James added, "And so, anytime I can't think of a name for something, I just use his simple approach. The robot is called Arthur – but it's really R-fer, meaning R-for robot."

An air hostess approached. "Excuse me, Mr. Moore? Dr. Peter Hammond is on the telephone. How are you feeling?"

James and Helen stared at each other in confusion, but Helen picked up and ran with the apparent joke faster than James. "He's feeling better, but I'm still a little concerned."

"The flight engineer has connected the call to your seat phone."

James removed the handset and waited for the attendant to leave. "Very funny, Pete…"

Pete interrupted forcefully. "This is no joke – have you cleared immigration and customs?"

Baffled. "Yes, in Dallas."

"Now listen carefully…"

Chapter 35

Although neither of them felt comfortable with the deception, Pete had convinced James that something was terribly wrong, and so they followed his instructions explicitly. As directed, they waited until the aircraft was in its final approach, and then James faked a strong stomach pain near his appendix. The flight crew had been pre-warned by Pete that the pressure change could aggravate James' already inflamed lower right intestinal tube, and if this occurred, they were to radio ahead and have an ambulance ready to rush him to the hospital.

According to plan, the instant the plane touched down and came to a complete stop, paramedics stormed aboard and immediately put James on oxygen and checked his vital signs. Much to his chagrin, they carried him off the plane on a stretcher, with Helen and the hand luggage in tow. Then, as directed shortly before arriving at emergency, James made a remarkable recovery, and as Pete had predicted he was instructed to remain in the waiting room until a doctor was free, since his condition was now no longer life threatening.

The deceit and humiliation of this masquerade had angered James beyond the point of caring about what he now believed was Pete overreacting. He could not for the life of him imagine what circumstances could have motivated him to go this far. Now fit to be tied, he paced the room oblivious to Helen's requests to calm down, raking his fingers through his hair.

By the time the slight, unshaven form of Pete appeared at the sliding glass door and beckoned for them to follow, James was about to explode. Dressed in an oversized jacket and a baseball cap that almost completely concealed his face and made him look ridiculous, he waved for them to follow and scurried towards a quiet, darkened area of the parking lot. Whisking up their bags, James marched over to Pete who was now holding open the rear passenger door, all the while looking nervously from left to right and signaled for them to hurry. Lobbing the bags onto the back seat, James pulled the door away from Pete, slammed it shut, and moved towards him aggressively, "What the hell do you think you're playing at?"

Pete was dumbfounded. "I'm saving your ass."

"Well, I'm about to kick yours," James yelled.

Eventually catching up with them, and noticing the heated confrontation, Helen intervened. "James, for God's sake give Pete a chance to explain... I'm sorry, Pete, but it's been a long flight and we're both tired and irritable – we just can't see why all this was necessary."

Pete lifted both hands in a gesture of supplication, "There's a lot of shit you don't know."

Taking a deep breath, James backed away slightly and seemed to be counting to ten before he responded. "I just want to know what on earth could have warranted this stupid farce."

"Okay, okay, I'll tell you... but it's not good news." Pausing, uncertain of where to begin, and reticent to continue, he said, "Somehow, we've stumbled on something that is so important to the people involved, that they are willing to kill to keep it a secret. I wish I'd caught you before you left... I would have told you not to come back."

Startled by the word 'kill', they stared at Pete, and it was only then that they noticed the lines of strain on his face. His fear and anxiety was contagious, and they were already dreading what he was going to say next. "Four heavily armed men, helped by two high ranking police officers I've known for years, tried to kill me last night… as you can see, by a stroke of luck, they didn't succeed."

Shaking her head in alarm Helen started to speak, but Pete lifted a hand, signaling that he hadn't finished. Looking down and shifting from one foot to the other, he searched for the best way to break the next piece of news, but as past experience had taught him, in cases like this, there is never an easy way. "Unfortunately, that's not all… I don't know how to tell you this, but… they did succeed in silencing your friend, James."

"What do you mean?" James' eyes were wide in apprehension and his mind raced to try and reason out what could have happened, all the while avoiding any path that would lead him to a place he did not want to go.

Pete's head dropped, unable any longer to look him in the eye and unwilling to continue. "I'm so sorry… but your friend Paul, his wife and their son are all dead… and I'm sure they were killed by the same people who tried to kill me."

"No… no… that's not possible," James stuttered, his voice hoarse with disbelief and shock. Stunned and shaken, he turned away and rested his arms on the roof of the car, as Pete relayed the few details he had been told by the fire inspector. Bowing his head, a feeling of unreality came over him and there was a sound of buzzing in his ears. Helen moved closer to him, tears running down her face, and placed a gentle hand on his shoulder,

"James…" she murmured, and as he turned slowly to look at them, they saw on his face an expression of not only sadness and shock, but moreover… guilt and remorse.

Culpability had not limited itself to only James' shoulders. For moments before, his friends had been alive and well in James' mind, and it seemed to Pete that in being the bearer of bad news, he himself, had effectively killed them.

Chapter 36

Distraught and weary, James had very little recollection of the next few hours. Like an automaton, he climbed into the back seat of the car, pulled on the seat belt and stared stone-faced out of the window. To him, the facts were plain and simple – he was directly responsible for their deaths. His brain felt numb and he liked it that way – he knew the pain would come eventually, but for the moment he did not want to think or feel.

The early morning commute had begun, and the reoccurring rhythm created by the oncoming cars was almost hypnotic, and seemed to encourage the silence. Helen sat close to him searching for those illusive words of comfort, that in matters of death were unobtainable. Then, a short, sharp blast on a car horn startled him out of his stupor, and catching a glimpse of Pete's eyes in the rearview mirror, he muttered hoarsely, "I owe you an apology, Pete." ·

"No, you don't."

"Yes, I do… I'm sorry for losing my temper back there."

Pete waited for a second, not wanting to go on, but knowing he had no choice. "I don't need an apology, James – what I really need right now is your focus. I know you've had a terrible shock. I've lived with this all day and had time to adjust to the situation. I don't want to sound callous, but we just haven't got the luxury of time – we've got to talk."

Sighing heavily, James slumped back in his seat and turned away again, staring mindlessly at the steady stream of traffic.

"Pete, I just don't think…"

Helen interrupted, "Look, Pete, can we talk about this later?"

"No, I'm sorry, Helen, we can't. I know what you're both thinking. You probably want to drop all this – let it go… Well, it's too late, that choice isn't available anymore… Don't you see, they think we know everything – whoever they are. Now as it happens, we don't. But that doesn't make any difference to them – we need to be removed from the picture because we pose too much of a threat." Glancing again in the mirror for any sign of a response, he noticed only Helen seemed to be listening. "…And don't think I'm saying all this because I want to avenge what happened to me or the deaths of your friends – I'm just trying to prevent mine, and yours."

"Well then, it's time we went to the police…" Helen said tersely, "…If we avoid the two men who betrayed you, we should be all right."

"Okay… fine… great… just don't turn your back on anyone while you're in protective custody, and don't count on NOT having a fatal accident before you get to talk to someone who gives a shit… All I can do is warn you that two high-ranking veteran police officers sold me out without a second thought. I don't know who else is working for them, but I don't trust anybody."

"Then, maybe we should go to the FBI and tell them everything we know."

"Okay, and what do we know, Helen. Have the two of you come up with any hard facts or evidence? Do we know who's involved and why?" He paused, and getting no reply, gestured with his head towards James. "I'll tell you something. I haven't known him for that long, but there's one thing I'm sure of, we need another plan – and he's the one to come up with it… C'mon

James! I know all about you, I pulled your file and read your military record. You've been under fire before… We need your help!"

Helen pleaded, "Pete, can't you wait until…"

Lifting his head from his hand, James interrupted, "It's okay, Helen, he's right… we really have to work together. I don't know how, but I'm going to have to put this out of my mind for the time being." It seemed he was not even going to be afforded the time to mourn his friends. Angry at the burning of unshed tears behind his eyelids, he rubbed his eyes roughly, desperately trying to push aside his emotions and replace them with cold hard logic.

"Okay… right… let me think for a minute." He paused as he cleared his throat and pulled himself together. "So… what do we have? Well, we have a multiple murder that has been made to look like an accident, an attempt on Pete's life which no one but Pete witnessed, and a folder filled with letters telling an interesting story from the past. Although I'm convinced the details from the past directly connect to the present, Pete's right, we have no evidence linking the people involved, to the present day crimes being committed… But I think I know where we can get it."

"Where?" Pete and Helen spoke in unison.

"Paul left me a message – it must have been the day before…" James stopped speaking, and then carried on his voice breaking slightly, "…he was killed. I think your two corrupt policemen and another man from the mayor's office, searched my office under the false pretense they were looking for details on a student. But, before leaving, Paul instructed a robot near to my office to covertly record their activities on its internal drive."

"And this robot would be able to do that?"

"Yes. It's an educational tool Paul and I designed and built to demonstrate technology... Now, they believed they were alone, so I'm hoping they might have mentioned something."

Arriving at Jim's house, Pete drove directly into the garage, stopped the car, and twisted around in his seat to face them. "Good... very good. When do you want to go pick it up?"

"I think it should be as soon as possible... tonight would be best. The administration staff leaves at five, and most of the security guards know me from night classes – so we should have no trouble. My card key is in my car, and so we'll have to pick it up first."

"Where's your car?"

"It's at the dealership downtown. It was due for its scheduled maintenance and so I left it with them while we were away. They dropped us to the airport."

"Brilliant, I'd never have thought of that. They probably searched everywhere for it and then gave up, assuming you must have taken it with you wherever you went."

"But James..." Helen sounded troubled, "...why don't we just go to Erik and talk to him about all this. Tell him everything, about the folder, the Mind Link – about seeing Karl. I mean, I've never really been that fond of him, but he is my uncle... I've always found him a little cool and aloof but I think that's just his personality. I've never known him to do anything really bad, and I certainly can't imagine him doing anything like this... this is probably all Karl List's doing – I've always thought he was creepy."

Not wanting to disillusion her, James chose his words carefully, "Let's just get the disc first love, then we can hopefully find out who we're up against and what their objective is. Until we have that, we're in the dark."

Looking deeply into James' eyes, she said unhappily, "But

you think Erik is at the heart of all this, don't you?"

"Well, I'm sorry, Helen, but everything we have seems to be centered around him... but let's keep an open mind until we're sure."

Jumping out of the car, Pete opened the car door and grabbed a couple of their bags. "You guys must be tired and hungry – come on in and make yourselves comfortable. There's nothing to eat and drink, so I'm going to zip down to the grocery store."

Unlocking the front door he placed the bags just inside, and switched on some lights. "Try and relax... I'll only be a few minutes." He turned to leave, then stopped abruptly in the doorway frowning as if he wanted to say something. James looked at him questioningly. Shuffling his feet he suddenly reached for James' hand and clasping it firmly, mumbled, "I'm sorry about your friends, Buddy... real sorry," and then hurrying through the door, closed it quietly behind him.

Chapter 37

The breakfast plates and cutlery had been stacked and pushed to one side of the dining room table to make room for the contents of the satchel and the laptop displaying Marlene's translated letters. Pete lolled back in his chair cracking his knuckles, listening intently as James and Helen reiterated their conversation with Colin Hawthorne. They had been running on reserve energy since their return, but now as the hours passed, they felt themselves beginning to fade. The draining emotions of the day together with the jet lag were finally taking their toll, and even the copious cups of coffee consumed were not able to ward off the onslaught of fatigue.

Pete noticed the telltale signs – the heavy heads, drooping eyelids, slightly slurred speech, and after seeing James shake his head for the second time in an effort to clear the fogginess, he broke in. "The two of you look beat – crash out on the bed and get some sleep. I'm going to do the same thing after I've read these letters."

"Are you sure, Pete?" questioned Helen running her hands through her hair, at the same time attempting to conceal a huge yawn.

"I'll be fine – and anyway, there's nothing for us to do now but wait for dark."

James rose up from his seat, "Okay, you're right… if we don't get some sleep, we won't make it this evening. C'mon, love."

They collapsed on the bed whereupon Helen immediately fell into a deep sleep, but James, unbelievably, could not even relax enough to drift off even though his eyes were burning and his head was pounding. The reason for this stemmed from the fact he had never been any good at letting things go. The fragmented pieces of the mystery kept swirling around in his head, and this distraction was hardly conducive to sleep. What frustrated him most was the obscure but unequivocal link between the past and the present.

Then, just as he was about to abandon the idea of sleep, he felt his mind slowly unwind and he began to slip into that twilight territory just before unconsciousness. It was in this region he had often found he was able to crystallize his thoughts, and as he mentally stepped back to view the broader canvas, the segments suddenly slotted into place. Although a few areas were still masked in shadow, the delineation conveyed enough information to theorize on the parts that were missing. The revelation was startling and his eyes sprang wide open, any vestige of fatigue discounted.

Leaping off the bed he ran into the living room, grabbed his laptop from in front of a sleeping Pete who had passed out in an armchair, and set about documenting his hypothesis. Piece after piece, the puzzle began to take shape. While Pete and Helen slept, James feverishly documented the details and clarified the connection between past and present. Several hours later he was finally satisfied, and after signing off and shutting down his computer, he crept into the bedroom. Depleted both physically and mentally, he sank down on the bed beside Helen and slipped easily into a deep sleep.

***

The telephone on the bedside table was of the old type that signaled incoming calls not with a gentle purr or pleasant warble, but with a resounding ring. Although it rang only once before Pete picked up the extension in the living room, the severity of the sound was a rude awakening, especially for James who had only been asleep for thirty minutes.

Dragging himself off the bed, he stumbled through to the living room and threw himself into the armchair. Pete, also looking worse for wear, sat hunched over the telephone. From what James could deduce from the muttered expletives, it was obvious to him that things had gone from bad to worse. There was a pause as Pete leaned forward and put his head in his hand, murmuring, "You're kidding me – I can't believe this crap!" Then finally, "Thanks, Sam… I can't thank you enough." Replacing the phone he sat there, stunned, his hand still resting on the receiver. His face was ashen and nervous perspiration made his shirt cling to his body, accentuating his thin, wiry torso.

"What is it, Pete?" James' voice sounded sharp with trepidation.

In a daze he turned and stared at James only just realizing he was there.

"Pete, what—"

Abruptly snapping out of his trance, Pete interrupted. "What a crock of shit!… James, listen, we've got to leave immediately. Get Helen and your things – I'll explain everything when we're out of here!" he yelled, rushing out to the garage to ready the car.

Within minutes of Sam's call, they were in the car and heading out of the neighborhood. Before they left, Pete had spent several minutes fervidly checking over the car, patently ignoring James and Helen's anxious pleas to let them know what was going on. It was only after driving away from the house, all the time looking nervously in the rearview mirror to check they were not being followed, that he felt safe enough to explain.

The caller was Sam Patterson, a fellow detective close to retirement and an old friend of his father's. He had called Pete from a call box to warn him the entire department had been mobilized to hunt him down. The evidence against him was overwhelming, and included a reliable witness who had identified Pete as the shooter in a gun battle with a drug dealer in which an innocent twelve-year-old girl had been killed in the crossfire. After apparently running from the scene, Pete was supposedly pursued by a squad car to his house, and in another engagement he critically wounded a police officer before escaping. A thorough investigation of his home uncovered a large quantity of cocaine with an estimated street value in excess of $1.3 million. Sam, believing in Pete's innocence and sensing this was some sort of set up, took the risk of trying to contact him.

Horrified, Helen leaned forward in her seat, "But... how did Sam know where you were?"

"He didn't, he knew my partner Jim was out of the country, and just put two and two together. I wouldn't have answered the phone, but I'd fallen into a deep sleep, and when it rang I just picked it up without thinking."

"Did he tell you anything else?"

"Just to get the hell out of there, because if he could work it out that easily, then so could they."

"I can't believe this is happening!" Helen exclaimed, dropping back into her seat. "What do you think, James?"

James smiled grimly, "I think it's a great move on their part. Why just have Erik's men looking for us when they can enlist the help of the entire police force... Did he give you any advice,

Pete?"

"Yeah, he told me to get across the border and wait until this whole thing calms down. He's going to do some digging and see what he can find."

"Sounds like good advice," James glanced at the time on the car's dashboard, which showed five-thirty, "The service center closes at five, but the cashier is there till seven. This is a little earlier than we planned, but I think we should first go and pick up my car and get rid of this one."

Pete concurred, "You're right, once they get to Jim's and find we've been there, they'll immediately have an APB out on this car."

***

It was dusk when James eventually pulled up alongside the security guards hut at the entrance to the University. On seeing James, Lou sauntered over and leaned on the ledge of the half door. "I thought it was you, Professor Moore... did you have a good Easter break?" he said, genuinely pleased to see James.

"Yes, thank you, Lou. How was yours?"

"Not so bad. Had to work, but I didn't mind so much," he answered congenially, and then lowering his voice and losing all his jocularity, he added, "I heard about Professor Barnes and his family... terrible thing that was. I'm going to miss him – he was a real nice man."

"Yes... Yes he was. I'm going to miss them very much too." James was holding onto his composure with a thread, and this heartfelt gesture loosened his grip momentarily and he looked away, his expression somber.

Realizing he had struck a raw nerve, Lou tried to compensate by changing the subject, "I'm about half way through your new book. It's great."

"Oh, thanks… I'm glad you're enjoying it."

He opened the half-door of the hut, and leaning down and peering in at Helen and Pete, he continued confidentially, "Whenever I'm on my rounds in the evening, I always like to sit in on his classes for a while." Inquisitive and amiable by nature, he carried on smiling and glancing between James and his friends.

"Oh… I'm sorry Lou, where are my manners. This is Helen and Pete. Pete, Helen… this is Lou – Night Security Officer and a good friend… Lou, would it be all right if we just pop in for a few minutes? I've got to pick up something."

"Oh sure, I'll let the security office know you're on the way… go right ahead." After activating the switch to open the barricade, he lifted a hand in a gesture of salute, and he called out, "Are you all prepared for next semester?"

"No… but then that's half the fun of it!" James replied as he drove off, leaving Lou laughing uproariously at his only halfway pithy comment.

Pulling into a car space at the rear entrance of the university, James climbed out and Pete slid into the driving seat. "Stay in the car with Pete, Helen, I won't be long."

"No, I'm coming with you," Helen said adamantly leaping out of the car and following James to the card reader.

"I'm going to park somewhere out of sight. Will you be coming out from this exit?" Pete called after them.

"Yes… we should only be about fifteen minutes."

***

Absent of the usual bustle and with only night lighting on, the long-darkened hallways and vacant offices and classrooms created an eerie atmosphere. The isolation felt menacing, and the silent echoing corridors emphasized the clatter of Helen's heels as she followed James to his office. Unlocking the door, he reached round for the switch, and after several flickers, the room flooded with light. In contrast to the dimness of the hallway the fluorescent strips were glaringly bright, and it took a moment or two for their pupils to adjust.

Void of any personality; the office looked stark and cold. A large wooden desk stood in the center, meticulously tidy, together with a comfortable-looking office chair. Against the wall were a couple of tall black metal filing cabinets, on which a selection of metal shelves had been haphazardly arranged, stacked with books and various batches of paperwork. An overhead fan came on with the lights, and it rotated listlessly, barely stirring the air.

In one corner, as expected, Arthur the robot sat on his recharging home pad. Electronic circuit boards were mounted on all sides of its cube shaped body, which rested on three wheels. Sensors mounted in the head assembly looked like the robot's eyes and ears, and a mechanical arm extended out in front, with a two-digit gripper at the end.

"Arthur," said James. Small lights on nearly all of the boards turned on, and it responded, its sharp robotic voice abrupt and abrasive, "Yes, sir, how can I help you."

Fascinated, Helen knelt down and scrutinized the robot. "Will he only answer to your commands?"

"Well, actually me and... Paul." Crouching down beside him he continued, "Arthur, eject read/write CD."

In response, a small drawer low to the ground, slid out revealing a compact disk, which James removed. Then, going over to his desk he inserted the disk into his desktop computer, sat down and waited for the system's start-up routine to complete. Opening the CD file, he looked through the list of contents displayed on the computer screen. "Ah, here it is," he said, clicking on a file Paul had created just days earlier.

Helen leaned forward and peered over his shoulder at the monitor as he fast-forwarded through the audio/video recording. "Good, good… Look at this, Helen! He got it, and it looks like they were in here for quite a while."

"Wait, WAIT… Go back!" she cried, squeezing James' shoulder urgently. Switching to rewind, James reversed the recording and played it back at normal speed. "There… see… THAT, is Karl List," she said, pointing to a man on the screen, shown entering James' office.

Both of them waited in silence as James increased the volume of the computer speakers. The two men rifling through James' desk looked up when Karl entered. "Two teams will carry out the Hammond and Barnes eradication tonight. The two of you will only be needed for the Hammond surveillance and confirmation. I will call you to give you further instructions," he said abruptly.

James grimaced and Helen lowered her head, appalled at what they were hearing. "It looks like we have them, Helen!" he said quietly.

"I can't believe he's such a vile and loathsome man."

"C'mon, let's go, I've seen all I want to see for now."

He was about to stop the playback and eject the CD, when he noticed one of the men climb onto his chair and reach up to the smoke sensor in the corner of his office. Studying the screen, he glanced quickly back at the detector. "…I know what you're going to do," he muttered, and dragging his chair over to the corner of the room, he climbed up and flipped open the sensor's cover. "DAMN!" he shouted, forcibly yanking out a miniature camera concealed within the unit, and throwing it against the wall.

"What is it, James?"

While removing the CD from the computer and slipping it into a protective case before he put it into his jacket pocket, he said, "Helen... they know we're here – we've got to go... Now."

Chapter 38

Leaving his office, they hurried back the way they came and were half way to the elevators when James stopped abruptly. "Let's not be so predictable – we'll use the other set of elevators." Taking Helen's hand, he pulled her in the reverse direction.

"But James, Pete is waiting at the main entrance."

"That doesn't matter, once we're out of the building we'll circle back to him."

The time they took traversing the length of the long corridor would have put a trained athlete to shame, and if there were an ideal moment for an elevator to be ready and waiting – this would be it! Unfortunately, it was not to be, and so they were forced to wait, impatiently listening to the distant whine of the electric motor hauling a cabin up to their floor.

The precipitant loud thump produced when the double-doors slammed shut echoed menacingly down the length of the passageway. Startled, they both turned instinctively to search the darkened corridor for the source of the disturbance. Relieved to see the familiar university security uniform, they sighed deeply and smiled at each other, slightly embarrassed at their over-reaction. Now familiar with the thud of the doors, they paid very little attention to the second occurrence, and if it wasn't for the fact they had nothing better to do but wait, they may not have glanced back at all. Fortunately for them, they did, for although they could only see an outline at the end of the long narrow passageway, it was enough to convince them the two men approaching were not guards.

Backing slowly and quietly away from the single low-wattage light above the elevators, James guided Helen into the small gap between two soda dispensers. From her cramped position behind him, she was able to see through the mesh of pipes and wires at the rear of the unit, while he peered around the front.

The two men marched quickly down the hallway in unison, using their flashlights to illuminate the nameplates on each office and classroom door as they passed. In his haste to leave, James had inadvertently left the light on in his office, and this glowed through the glass like a beacon, directing the men to the exact location they were searching for. Taking up a position either side of the door, they drew their handguns, kicked open the door shattering the pane, and stormed in with their guns extended.

With them now out of sight, Helen turned to James and whispered, her voice taut with fear, "James, what are we going to do?"

He squeezed her hand comfortingly trying to contain her fear. "Stay calm, Helen, they'll leave now they think we're not here."

Minutes passed and they remained immobile in their confined space, acutely aware any movement could reveal their whereabouts. Eventually, both men reappeared, holstered their weapons, and stared up and down the corridor. The slimmer of the two then lifted his hand to his ear and appeared to activate a transceiver.

It was at this time the security guard James and Helen had seen earlier rounded a corner, having returned to investigate the loud percussive noise generated when the office door was forced open. As he approached, he could see the broken glass scattered across the floor, and assuming the accident was unintentional, asked in congenial a manner, "What happened here, then?"

His initial question was merely perfunctory, but after receiving no reply he repeated it – only this time louder. The absence of a response again left no doubt in his mind the two men had no intention of answering him, and this was confirmed by their body language that conveyed an arrogance and implied he was of no consequence.

Confused at their reticence and angry at their insolence he tried again, raising his voice aggressively. "Excuse me gentleman, have you checked in at the security office?" His inquiry was again discounted, and now extremely irritated he reached for his radio and stated authoritatively, "Right, I'm going to have to call this in, and we will see what we will see."

This action got their attention, and turning quickly to face him, the thinner of the two operatives moved his hand rapidly towards his hip. For a few tense seconds they both froze, the guard with his hand on his radio still clipped to his belt, and the operative with his hand hovering over the handle of his still holstered handgun. In the blink of an eye, the gun cleared the holster, was brought quickly up to eye level, and fired at point blank range summarily executing the guard with a single shot to the head.

James twisted around and was just able to get a hand over Helen's mouth, in time to muffle her cry of disbelief. Pulling her into his chest, he could see her wide-open eyes well up with tears and feel her breathing quicken. Leaning back and turning his head to the side, he studied the two men who seemed to have received new instructions, and were now walking in their direction.

Pushing Helen further back against the wall he looked for a

path of escape that would not be visible. Then, as if to draw further attention to them, the elevator chose this particular time to arrive with a piercing "ding" as the door opened. Crammed as they were behind the soda dispensers, they were not able to see clearly, so James had to be content with what he could ascertain from the nearby sounds. Listening avidly, he heard the footsteps stop, a shuffle and then silence, and assumed the two men were aiming their guns into the empty elevator. After what seemed like an interminable wait, they strode into the elevator, only momentarily coming into his immediate view. As soon as the door closed, James pulled Helen out of their hiding place and back towards his office.

"Where are we going, James?" she asked, her voice trembling uncontrollably.

"Back to my office... Don't worry, they've already checked there and so we'll be safe for a while."

Back in the office, Helen sat slumped in the chair, numb with shock. It had taken all her strength to step around the bloody corpse of the slain guard, and she leaned forward and wept silently into her hands. Thrusting aside his own feelings of aversion, James had groped around the inert body hoping his radio and gun had been left, but the two operatives had obviously appropriated these items offering James no means of communication or defense. He paced the floor, his mind searching feverishly for a way to evade their pursuers. Then, an idea struck him, and stopping mid-stride he turned, darted back to the computer and began to type. A few moments later, Arthur burst into life and all at once began an initializing process, cycling through each of his motors and sensors, testing each to see if they were all fully functional.

Startled out of her misery, Helen turned and stared dully at the activated robot. James knew they had no time to waste and he needed to jolt her into action. He grabbed both her hands and pulled her out of the chair. "Helen, listen... Helen... are you listening?" Taking her by the shoulders, he shook her slightly. "We've got to go – they're after us... Now follow me quickly."

Entering the corridor, he used his foot to flick down the latch on the bottom of the door so it stayed wide open. He did the same thing to all the double doors and classroom doors on that floor. Helen followed him blindly and when they had traveled full circle and returned to his office, her curiosity finally got the better of her, and she asked, "What on earth are you doing?"

"Giving them something to chase. Hopefully it will give us time to get away... okay, I think this looks good – let's go."

Satisfied with his plan, he took Helen to an invalid ramp that led up to the next floor, explaining as they went, "Arthur is going to distract them for a while. They came straight to my office hoping to find us both there, which we weren't. They headed down in the elevator, so my guess is they're going to start on the first floor and move up checking each floor one by one... meanwhile, you and I will be leaving."

***

Marching through the main entrance of the university, Karl beckoned over a senior operative to brief him of the situation. The thug-like man, restless and sweating profusely, pointed in the direction of the corridors. "We have all the main exits covered, but the University is very large and we would need a lot more men to secure all the possible paths. We're quite sure they are still in the building and we're preparing to do a floor-by-floor search."

"If you need more personnel bring in surveillance and electronic units, but lock it up tight – I don't want them slipping through."

"I'll bring them in immediately, sir."

"What about the elevators?"

"All disabled, sir."

Karl stalked into the Security Office and, with callous indifference, shoved a dead security guard off the chair. Sitting down and swiveling slightly from side to side, he studied the surveillance monitors. "These cameras only cover the first floor and immediate perimeter – is that correct?"

"Yes, sir."

"Right, let's get going. Send up two men to the second floor. Tell them that Mr. Moore may be armed and not to underestimate him. Have the others maintain their positions at the exits. I will personally respond when they are detected."

When they arrived back at the second floor via the stairs, the same two operatives were immediately alerted by the corridor's changed appearance. Doors that had been closed were now open, exposing them to many angles of attack, and somewhere ahead in the shadows, a strange indeterminate sound emanated. Uneasy, they held their position and radioed for backup. "Somebody's been here since we checked it last, and there are noises coming from the other end of the hallway."

"Hold fast – I'll be right there," responded Karl in anticipation.

Reaching their position, Karl paused, and frowning, turned his head to one side attempting to decipher the sporadic noises coming from the far end of the corridor. Removing an antique Luger from his belt holster, he drew the slide back and released it to chamber the first round. His ice-blue eyes glinted, and turning towards the men he said with an uncharacteristic smile, "I will cover the right side, you take the left, and you watch our rear... Gentlemen, let the games begin!"

Systematically and methodically, they moved down the corridor, checking every room. Their defensive tactics and attention to detail made for slow going and the echoing effect in the hall seemed to bounce the sounds around making it difficult to pinpoint a direction. The noises seemed to always be coming from around the next corner, and in a short time they had circled the entire floor and returned to their original position – their prey still eluding them.

"Hold on..." said Karl, sensing something was not quite right, and after a moment's thought added, "...follow my lead." Reversing direction, he stretched his handgun out in front of him and took off at a brisk pace heading for the source of the disturbance, which now seemed to be coming from behind them. Alert and anxious, his two cohorts felt extremely vulnerable as they marched directly towards a possible threat. When they reached a turn and could hear their enemy almost upon them, they both held back, tensing themselves for the confrontation. Karl, on the other hand, charged straight ahead with no break in his stride, turned the corner at full speed, entered one room, and then another. Knowing the dire consequences that would result if they did not accompany him, the subordinates set out in hot pursuit and found him, gazing in amazement at Arthur, who was running a program James and Paul had devised called 'hide and seek'.

Sensing an obstacle blocking the path in front of him, Arthur turned off his sonar navigation system and switched to his infrared motion sensor in order to confirm he had indeed been found by a warm-body. After verification, he announced in his staccato voice, "You win, but your time was poor... now, you go and hide and I will seek."

Looking down at his errant quarry, Karl slowly nodded his head approvingly, "Bravo, Mr. Moore... A worthy adversary at last."

Chapter 39

Bursting through the double-doors, they entered another dimly lit corridor. After searching the length of the hallway and seeing no one, James grabbed Helen's hand and pulled her towards a side door marked EXIT. Through the small eye-level window in the door they could see a staircase going both up and down.

"Hold on a second," said James trying to catch his breath, all the while listening for anyone approaching. Resting her back up against the wall, Helen lowered herself to the floor, and put her head in her hands.

"I don't understand…" she said through tears. "Are they trying to kill us?"

Looking down at her, he reached for her hand and pulled her back up and towards him, "I don't know, love – but don't worry, I'll get us out of this." His eyes were wide and alert, and his mind raced through any and all possibilities. "We've got to get to the University's security office on the first floor. We could take these back stairs, but…" he paused.

"But what?"

"…Somehow I know, this is exactly what they expect us to do."

Clenching his fist and tapping it lightly against his chin, he closed his eyes in concentration. "Fire escape – of course… quick Helen, this way."

Through the door to the stairway, he led her up to the fourth floor, and then to the fifth. As they entered, an elated shout came from the stairs below, "They're on this set of stairs, and heading up."

Running half way down the corridor, James pulled Helen through a set of large doors leading into a lab. Weaving their way through a maze of large wooden tables laden with equipment to a door marked Emergency Exit, he whispered, "Stand right here and it's VITAL you don't move... We're going to need a diversion."

Helen watched as he activated a large switch on a wall panel and in response all of the equipment in the lab lit up. Moving around the room he turned on certain instruments and adjusted the position of others.

"What are we going to do, James?"

"Don't MOVE," he snapped aggressively.

"I haven't... but can you tell me what you're doing?"

"The staircase behind you is a fire exit, and it leads directly to the parking lot. This is the industrial technology lab. About two years ago I worked on the course curriculum, and taught the first few classes—"

His explanation was interrupted by the sound of voices and footsteps from the corridor. Stopping, he latched open both doors and worked his way back to Helen following what appeared to be an erratic path, and then lifting a bench stool high above his head, hurled it across the room so that it crashed through the doorway and careened into the corridor. Pushing open the emergency fire exit door, he turned to Helen. "Trust me... I know what I'm doing. If I can just get them off balance, we stand a better chance of slipping away. Now, go quickly, I'll be along shortly, I promise." Gripped with fear she began descending the spiral metal staircase anchored to the outside of the building while James held the Emergency Exit door slightly ajar, so he could see the entrance to the lab.

At that moment two men took up positions either side of the doorway, their guns drawn. Although it was dark in the corridor and James was unable to see clearly, their silhouettes distinctly revealed one of the men as tall and over-weight while the other was short and wiry. One spoke, "Can you see them, Brian?"

"No, Bob, you?"

"Nah… I can't see shit from here. See if I'm clear."

A head poked in the doorway, "You're clear."

Bob swung himself around and into the room, his gun extended, and it was at this time the light from the equipment exposed James' position. Seeing he was unarmed, Bob rushed towards him, followed immediately by Brian. Midway across the room, for no apparent reason, Bob appeared to trip and fall. Brian, a few paces behind, suddenly stopped dead in his tracks transfixed in shock at what he saw in front of him. With mounting horror he realized his partner and friend had been severed at the waist, and his body lay in two halves separated by an ever-expanding pool of blood. The scene was made even more horrific by the hideous consciousness of Bob, who leaned up on his hands and gazed with disbelief at the disconnected lower half of his body. Staring at Brian helplessly, his mouth opened in a desperate plea, but the final cry was trapped by the stroke of death. While Brian stood over him immobilized by shock, Karl arrived at the entrance to the lab, and quickly assessing the gruesome scene shouted, "Don't move… you're in the middle of a laser lab, those beams are invisible."

Turning away, sick with guilt, James hurried down the stairs and caught up with Helen. Peering into the darkness, he scoured the parking lot for any sign of Pete and his car. "Come on, where the hell are you?" he muttered under his breath. Then, seeing the headlights flash twice, he shouted, "There he is, let's go!"

Mustering up all remaining energy, they made a dash towards the car that was already speeding towards them. As the gap narrowed, however, James felt a sinking sensation come over him - even from this distance he could tell the sound of the engine and the body shape wasn't right. "That's not Pete, run to the right Helen!" he yelled veering off and heading towards a thicket of trees.

Seeing their change in course, the car switched on its high-beam headlights, accelerated, and quickly caught up to them. Two warning shots were fired to purposely hit directly in their path, and the violence with which they ricocheted off the tarmac forced them to stop with a jolt. Turning to face their pursuers who had screeched to a halt, they could just see the outline of a man with a gun through the glare of the headlights. "Dead or alive, Mr. Moore... the choice is yours."

Chapter 40

Within minutes, a swarm of vehicles surrounded them. Two men searched them, bound their hands behind their backs, and hustled them into the back of a black van with heavily tinted windows. A bulky guard with black slicked-back hair sat facing them, humming an indistinguishable tune rather loudly – and then their transport pulled away, the center vehicle in a five-car convoy.

In the dim interior James could plainly see the terror on Helen's face, and edging closer he murmured, his lips barely moving, "Don't worry, love… this is a good sign."

"I can't see it is."

"It would have been easier just to kill us, they seem to want us alive for some reason."

"And what would that be?"

"I haven't had a chance to tell you, but I think I've worked it out when you were asleep at Jim's house. Now, I want you…"

"No talking," the guard butted in lethargically.

Luckily at that time, they were all distracted by a change in their escort. Acknowledging new instructions, the driver changed lanes and fell in behind a large limousine, while the rest of their consort broke formation and withdrew. Taking advantage of this distraction, James continued. "Now listen carefully, Helen, in case I don't have a chance to say any more. Don't worry because I have a way for us to get out of this – my only concern was I wouldn't be given the chance to negotiate. But it looks like we're going to get that chance."

Unconvinced, she turned away and slumped back in her seat, staring out of the window into the gloom. His words had done nothing to alleviate her awful fear and apprehension. Closing her eyes, she pressed her forehead against the window, trying desperately to suppress the rising tide of panic. After a few minutes she opened them again, and immediately sat upright when she noticed they were approaching her home – the Banner estate. Stopping momentarily at the gates, then passing through, they swept up the driveway, and pulled up smoothly behind the limousine.

"So, it looks like you were right after all, James – it seems Eric is involved in all this," she said despondently as the van door opened. While they were being conducted out, an older man exited the limousine and marched steadfastly into the house without so much as a glance in their direction.

"Karl List, I presume?" James asked, turning to Helen.

"Yes. That's him."

Taking them by the arm, two guards led them into the house. "Let me do the talking Helen, and follow my lead. I know you're very upset and frightened. I'm going to get us out of this, but you're going to have to trust me."

"I do – completely," she replied with a wintry smile.

Feeling a little more positive now she was in her own home, Helen looked around eagerly, hoping for some sign of Maria – but the lights were off and the house was cold and lifeless. Escorted into the large drawing room they were instructed to sit on a love seat that had been positioned to face two winged armchairs, separated by a coffee table. A small table lamp giving out an inadequate amount of light, threw shadows into the darkened corners of the expansive room.

When Karl entered, the atmosphere became charged and the

two guards stood quickly to attention. James and Helen, who had been talking together softly, stopped abruptly and stared in amazement at this extraordinary display of outmoded military showmanship. Then, one of the men reached into his pocket and pulling out the optical disk, handed it over to Karl. "Here's the CD we retrieved from Mr. Moore, sir."

"Good. You may both leave. Tell the men they can take a break in the kitchen. Have the housekeeper prepare them what they want, but maintain a guard at the front of the house."

"Understood. Thank you, sir."

When they had left and closed the door behind them, Karl put the CD in his briefcase and sat in one of the armchairs. Making himself comfortable, he then removed a file and proceeded to read it, completely ignoring their presence.

"Good evening," James said politely, leaning back and trying to appear as comfortable as possible, even though his hands were tied behind his back.

Karl lifted his head only slightly in surprise, amused at the formality of the greeting, and with a sneer replied, "Good evening."

"I assume we're waiting for... Mr. Banner?"

"Your assumption is correct."

"Good, very good... and how would you prefer I address you?"

Lowering the file, Karl paused thoughtfully for what seemed like an inordinately long time. "Mr. List will be fine, Mr. Moore."

"As you wish... it's just that... well, I wasn't sure whether you wanted to be called Karl List... or Kurt Dietl!"

Helen swung her head around and gaped at James, her eyes wide with surprise. Karl's jaw had clenched tightly, his eyes fixed a cold stare on James and for a moment he seemed to lose his composure. In a warning voice he said, "I would keep quiet if I were you Mr. Moore, otherwise... I may decide to terminate this encounter before it has even begun."

James at first appeared to have heeded the warning, but then, leaning forward in his seat, he added conversationally, "...But then wouldn't you be overstepping your position? I mean... after all, you're only the guardian."

Chapter 41

Provoking their captor seemed a slightly unorthodox negotiation technique, but Helen was sure James had his reasons for choosing this tact. With their eyes now locked in a battle of wills, she felt a tightening of her muscles as she glanced back and forth between them. Karl's thin veneer of civility was finally slipping to reveal his true temperament – that of a violent, unstable man, lacking in any compassion or restraint. James, on the other hand, appeared extremely calm and relaxed, a fact that seemed to further antagonize Karl.

The aggrandizing tension was dispelled the moment Erik swept into the room. Karl rose quickly from his seat, hurried to meet him, and they turned away for a moment to confer privately. James could see the strain in the set of Karl's shoulders, as he muttered in German, clenching his fist and pounding it into the palm of his hand to emphasize his points. Eventually, they took their seats opposite them and James once again took the initiative, "Good evening."

"Helen, Mr. Moore," Erik said calmly in response, a slight supercilious smile touching his lips.

"Now… before we begin. Helen and I are going to find it very difficult to have a conversation, with our arms tied up in this uncomfortable position."

"Of course… Karl, would you mind?"

Karl, who had been nonchalantly brushing non-existent pieces of fluff from his jacket sleeve, stopped and stared at Erik aghast, and it was obvious to them he was struggling with this request. Erik looked back at him questioningly, and tension filled the room once again. Then, begrudgingly, Karl abruptly got up and strode across the room, removed a penknife from his pocket, and expertly cut off the restraints.

"Thank you…" said James, rubbing his wrists, "…now, I believe you have something you wanted to say?"

Erik again smiled, and after a delay asked caustically, "And why would you think that?"

"Because if you didn't… we wouldn't be here."

Leaning back in his seat, Erik raised his eyebrows slightly, "Mmm… Well, we do seem to have got ourselves into a bit of a predicament, don't we?"

"Yes… but not one we can't get ourselves out of."

"Really? You think so?"

"Certainly, as long as we are both willing to come to an arrangement."

"An arrangement? This is very interesting – pray, please continue, Mr. Moore, you have my undivided attention."

"Thank you. Now, you and Mr. Dietl here have tried very hard to conceal a secret I am now fully aware of…"

Karl, at this time, had meandered to the perimeter of the room, well away from the light, where it was impossible to read his facial expressions. His body reaction however was easy to interpret, when in response he swung around furiously, "You are in no position to bargain with us!"

Erik calmly raised his hand and shook his head slowly, silencing Karl's objections. He then signaled for James to proceed.

"… As I was saying, you have a secret that in and of itself is not criminal, however, the means and methods you have used to conceal it most definitely are. Helen and I, on the other hand, would prefer to stay out of harm's way – and so this is what I think you should do." While looking at his watch, he added with finality to his tone, "You and your Guardian now have exactly six hours and twenty-five minutes to leave the country – I would suggest South America as a destination."

Karl lowered his head, shook it in frustration and muttered, "…Warum machen wir nicht Schluss mit ihnen, sie sind eine Bedrohung, bringen wir sie beide um – selbst wenn sie deine Tochter ist."

Erik spun his head violently in Karl's direction and although no words were spoken, the meaning was perfectly clear. When he turned back, James could see the remnants of fury still upon his face, but he quickly composed himself. "Now this is fascinating, and I might add, intriguing. You want me to leave the country, and presumably never come back… otherwise you will do… what?"

"Last night I spent over four hours documenting your secret, and the methods you have employed to preserve it. This detailed report, which is supported by scanned letters, photographs, and other records, has been uploaded into a secret location on the internet and is addressed to twenty of the nation's top newspapers and magazines. I have attached a timer to it…" and looking again at his watch, he finished with, "…you now have six hours and twenty-two minutes to leave the country."

"I see… and you really think they'll believe you?"

"Maybe, maybe not… but can you afford to take the risk?"

From his winged chair, Erik regarded James with a mocking expression, making it patently clear he took none of this seriously. "I suppose you wouldn't mind telling me, just for curiosity's sake, the basic content of this article?"

"Of course not... as long as you don't mind losing the time?"

"I'm in no rush, Mr. Moore..." he gibed with a sarcastic laugh, "...in fact, where are my manners. Karl, have Maria prepare us some coffee."

"This is ludicrous I tell you..." Karl expostulated, his fragile composure disintegrating.

"Karl..." Erik said calmly, not moving or even glancing in his direction, "...I really must insist you order coffee, at once, please." His words were precise and carefully enunciated, and it was apparent to all his request was now an order. This, somehow, seemed to have the desired effect, and Karl picked up the nearby telephone.

"While we're waiting, please start?"

"Thank you, shall I start with your guardian?"

"If you wish."

"Mr. Karl List's real name is Kurt Dietl. He attended the Ordensburg College when he was a teenager during the Second World War, and was in the same class as Helga Kluge. I have a wonderful class photograph taken in 1943, showing the two of them... His grades and unquestioning obedience, no matter how ruthless the task, won him favor and he was summoned to Berlin in 1944 to guard Helga's child. She was also an excellent student, and felt honored to have been picked for the selective breeding program in which she was matched with a very... high-ranking official. After the boy was born, Kurt was instructed to remove Helga who had become disgruntled, in order to protect the father's identity, and he was then ordered to escort the boy to Argentina in a U-boat. The Fahnenbrueder, now relocated, searched for an influential adoptive parent in the U. S. – the only nation with its infrastructure still in place and destined to be the next super power. Hugh Banner met the criteria. Kurt Dietl, now renamed Karl List, waited until the boy was older before reestablishing contact. In 1973, Helga finally found her son and contacted Hugh Banner. For glimpsing the secret, Mr. List killed them both, and then the detective David Hammond, and Helen's mother…"

For the entire time Helen had said nothing, just sat almost motionless in her seat staring first at James, and then turning slowly towards Erik.

Feigning a look that deliberately blended interest with confusion, Erik asked, "Now let me try and follow this… you're saying this child… is…?"

"You."

"Oh, I see."

"Now, I could tell you a lot more, but that would only decrease your escape time, which is now… five hours and forty-five minutes."

Erik scoffed, "Oh please, don't concern yourself with the time. Entertain me further, Mr. Moore."

"This is no game Mr. Banner… your attempt to appear confused and innocent, while at the same time being interested, is patently clear. Well, I think it should be obvious to you by now I know enough, and that your best course of action would be for you and your sociopath toady to simply walk away… while you still have the chance."

The tableau froze and for a tense moment Karl, Helen and James stared wordlessly towards Erik, awaiting his response. This linguistic battle may have appeared a lot more civilized than a duel – but the stakes were still the same.

Rising slowly, Erik strolled round to the back of his chair and paused with his hand in his pocket, a deep frown etched in his handsome face. It was evident from his sudden change in demeanor he didn't appreciate James' direct approach, and said coldly and thoughtfully, "We have underestimated you right from the start Mr. Moore... but for the sake of argument, let's say I accept your story. If I'm the person you think I am, and Mr. List is this Kurt Dietl, why wouldn't we have killed the two of you the moment we caught you."

"Now, that's a good question, and one that has eluded me until this evening. I believed at first we were apprehended instead of being killed because you wanted to find out exactly how much we knew. But, this was not the real reason."

"It wasn't?"

"No... the real reason was revealed by your henchman this evening, who stupidly assumed I didn't understand German. Now, as it happens, I don't speak it very well, but I can get by... I think you should tell Helen, don't you? It may be better coming from you?"

Erik didn't move a muscle, and for the first time it looked as though James had found a chink in his armor, for he seemed to be at a complete loss for words.

A sensation of dread engulfed Helen, and she knew without a doubt she wasn't going to like what she was about to hear. Rising from her seat, she demanded, "Someone tell me what's going on – James, if Erik won't tell me, then you tell me... please!"

Grabbing her hand, he pulled her back down next to him and seeing Erik's reticence, he carefully worded his explanation. "Okay, I'm sorry you have to find out this way, but... Roughly translated, 'Warum machen wir nicht Schluss mit ihnen, sie sind eine Bedrohung, bringen wir sie beide um – selbst wenn sie deine Tochter ist' means, 'Why continue this, they are a threat, eliminate them both – even if she is your daughter'."

Chapter 42

Escorted by a guard, Maria entered the drawing room and was immediately taken aback by the highly charged tension generated by the occupants. Walking slowly with the heavily laden tray she made her way cautiously towards the dimly lit center. At the far side of the room a shaft of moonlight shone through the windows, its silvery glow illuminating Karl like a specter. Startled by his eerie presence, a shiver ran down her spine as she lowered the tray, and the china and silverware chinked together piercingly.

"Where is your husband, Maria, we can't seem to find him anywhere?" Erik asked pleasantly.

"He's in Mexico – his mother sick."

"Oh dear, I'm sorry to hear that, I hope she'll recover soon. Ah… coffee, thank you, Maria. Perhaps you would be kind enough to serve everyone." James studied this smooth shift in persona – this easy charm… so easily turned on when needed, so appealing to the general public he thought as Erik smiled benignly. So deceiving, so… dangerous!

"Not for me," Karl called out belligerently.

Setting out the cups, Maria looked up at Helen trying to catch her eye. Smiling at her reassuringly she noticed Helen's eyes fill with tears and trickle slowly down her cheeks. Disturbed at seeing her so distressed, she gently squeezed her arm in passing as she handed the coffee around.

Noticing this small gesture of affection, Erik said sharply, "That will be all, thank you, Maria."

Maria picked up a cup filled with coffee, and carrying it carefully with both hands, pottered over to Karl, her eyes downcast. Spinning round, any vestige of manners now defunct, he blared, "I said I didn't want any... don't you listen, you stupid imbecile."

This was the final straw for Helen – the unspeakable horrors of the day together with this humiliation of her beloved Maria snapped her restraints, and she turned on Karl like a tigress. "Don't you ever, ever speak to her like that again... do you hear... you... you disgusting BIGOT!" Her rage purged any sadness from her voice – the anger felt good, it flooded through her system, somehow cleansing her and making her feel stronger. Maria stood there passively, and a guard, keen to defuse the tension, hurried over and bustled her out of the room.

During the whole interaction Erik had sat calmly observing the proceedings. Picking up his cup, he reclined back into his chair and crossed one well-tailored leg over the other. Lifting the spoon from the saucer he began a slow stir that was periodically interrupted when he raised the spoon out of the cup and tipped it to watch the steaming brew trickle back into the cup with a plopping sound. "Well, well, well... the worm has finally turned – I didn't know you had it in you, Helen," he declared approvingly, taking a long satisfying sip of coffee. "I don't know why you're in such a state. There was nothing wrong – it wasn't as if your mother and I were related by blood. It just happened – she should have been more careful."

Helen turned away in disgust. "I don't believe it."

"But it's the truth. Your birth certificate lists your father as unknown, but that was your grandfather's idea – he didn't want the scandal."

"My mother said she was engaged to a navy flier who was

219

killed in the Vietnam War."

"Yes. Convenient, wasn't it?"

Her mind raced in disbelief, as she tried to find some memory that would erase this shocking revelation. "And why haven't you told me in all these years?"

"Because, I didn't want any part of it... I had my own agenda, and you were not part of the plan. I told your mother I wanted nothing to do with you. Actually, I was hoping when your mother married that Thompson guy I'd get you both out of my hair – but that only lasted a couple of years and then you were both back on the estate."

"What a nasty piece of work you are," she said bitterly.

"Insulting me seems pointless. You know... you're a little old to be playing the role of the rejected child."

James had said nothing, just listened throughout this altercation, but he now butted in, "Your logic seems a little muddled, Mr. Banner – you claim to feel no emotional attachment to Helen, and yet you must have instructed your men to capture her unharmed. Now why would that be?"

Emotion was not something that Erik ever acknowledged, and it aggravated him immensely to be cornered in this way. Putting his cup down carefully, he rose from his seat, and moving behind it, leaned on the back. "I'm beginning to wonder that myself," he said slowly, almost to himself.

Still seething, Helen flicked her head up to face him and added with undisguised loathing, "I should thank you... I can see that I benefited greatly from having no involvement with you at all. As far as I'm..."

With an expression of boredom, Erik interrupted her, "Do you mind if we get back on track." Out of the corner of his eye, James could see Helen about to carry on and immediately squeezed her hand gently, shaking his head slightly.

"Of course," he said politely, deliberately looking once again at his watch.

Seeing this intentional gesture, Erik smiled caustically. "I'll admit, this timed-release article idea of yours is a good one... is it meant to intimidate me?"

James shook his head in disgust, "You seem to treat all of this like it's a game of chess, and that my sole objective is to try and get the better of you... well it's not, and I'm not – my only motive is to try and save Helen, myself, and any other poor soul that accidentally happens to stumble on your past. I don't even think I should be letting you go, but I can't do much about that. The only thing I'm sure about is that you need to be stopped, and removed from any position of power."

Pushing himself away from the chair, Erik chuckled, "It seems the majority of the voters in this city would disagree with you."

"At this particular moment in time, yes – but let's see how their opinions change when I introduce them to the warped, callous and evil mind concealed behind that outwardly presentable and civilized manner."

Sighing heavily, he retorted, "I see no point in continuing this." He had clearly had enough and walked over to Karl, who stood with his back to them, looking out of the window.

As they conversed quietly together James took the opportunity to whisper, "Now listen, Helen... I have something else I can use to apply more pressure, but I'm afraid it might backfire on us."

Visibly shaken, she replied tremulously, "At this stage, James, I think anything is worth a try. Frankly, I think they're capable of anything, and I don't know how much more time we have."

Nodding at her, he looked over at the two men talking, and called out loudly, "To help you in your decision I feel I should also make you aware of another important fact that is described in the article."

Karl spun around, but Erik continued looking out of the window. "And what's that?" he asked, his voice dangerously low.

"Helga's diary was hidden but survived. During the selection process, Helga talked about a young woman, named Miss Eva, who competed against her and controlled the testing. It took me a while to make the connection, but then I worked out who your father was."

Erik turned slowly towards them – fortunately for him the darkness in the corner of the room concealed the look of alarm that swept across his face. Neither he nor Karl said a word – they just stood there, the meager light throwing their shadows into grotesque shapes on the opposite wall.

"I know everything…" James carried on. "It all fell into place late last night when I was working on the article, going over and over the letters. History states Eva was sterile, and so a young girl that matched her looks, intellect and physical abilities was chosen to be a surrogate mother. Why would they marry towards the end of the war if they had no future together? They married and escaped to Argentina in exactly the same way you did – on a U-boat."

Erik finally spoke, "I'm afraid you've overplayed your hand."

"But don't you see. Even if you couldn't be convicted on any of the other charges, you wouldn't stand a chance in politics, or anything else in this country for that matter, once the truth is known. Your secret is going to be plastered across every newspaper and magazine in the country, and around the world…

and so, why make matters worse and do something you'll regret – surely you must see your best option is to walk away."

"You know… you're a fine speaker, Mr. Moore, and I must say I'm pleased you're not in politics… Now, as far as your offer is concerned, I'm going to have to decline… I've come much too far to walk away, and I have plans to go a lot further. Politicians have suffered worse setbacks than this – and I think…" He shook his head and blinked his eyes as though he was having trouble focusing, "…You'll find the only publications that will be interested in… your article… will be the tabloids. We've wasted enough time, Karl, you were right… I think… we should…"

They all looked at Erik incredulously as his speech slurred, he swayed back and forth as though heavily inebriated, and then slumped to the floor. In that instant, the French doors leading to the dining room were kicked open violently, and Pete suddenly appeared pointing a gun at Karl. Reacting quickly, Karl flipped over a heavy side table and ducked down behind it. James grabbed Helen, and jamming his heels heavily into the floor, forced the love seat to flip backwards, providing a barricade and removing them from harm's way. To halt Pete's advance, Karl lifted his gun so it cleared the top of the table, and took a few wild shots at Pete, who immediately dropped to the floor. The tactic worked and Pete slipped behind one of the winged chairs for protection. "He's behind that table – keep the shotgun pointed over there. If you get a shot, take it," Pete yelled to a stranger who had followed him in and was sidestepping to the right attempting to outflank Karl.

Realizing he was outmanned and outgunned, Karl picked up a large marble ornament that had fallen from the table and hurled it through the window directly behind him. Then, lifting the table and using it as a shield, he clambered through and disappeared into the darkness of the night.

Chapter 43

James felt his surroundings take on an air of surrealism as he watched Helen leap up and run into the arms of the man with the shotgun. Then, as if in slow motion, Pete turned and walked towards him, at the same time extending his hand to help him up. Yanking him to his feet, he slapped James amiably on the shoulder, and then assuming a baffled expression said jokingly, "What was the plan James – were you trying to talk him to death? I swear... You English."

"Emm, yes... I mean, no... how did you know where we were?"

Pete's explanation was interrupted by Maria, who came tearing into the room calling, "Helen, Helen, Helen!" And engulfed Helen in a suffocating bear hug. Tears of relief were streaming down her beaming face, and when she finally released her, it was only to frantically search her frame for any signs of injury "Are you okay, my sweetie?"

"I'm fine, Maria, really... thank God you all came when you did."

Witnessing their touching reunion seemed to inspire Pete to put his arm around James' shoulder in a friendly fashion, evidently much moved by the sudden outpouring of emotion. This was not in any way a comfortable pose as Pete was almost a head shorter than James, and so a stretch was required on his part. Crouching slightly to accommodate this unexpected expression of goodwill, James felt he should somehow respond and so lifted his arm towards his shoulder. This, however, seemed to put undue strain on Pete's balance, and so he had to be satisfied with simply resting his arm on his waist and nodding congenially. Pete seemed content to maintain this uncomfortable posture, but James by this time was feeling utterly ridiculous. Deciding to employ a question as a means of escape, he slowly slid out from under Pete's arm, patted him several times on the shoulder to acknowledge this heart-felt gesture, and said, "Thanks a lot, Pete... but how the hell did you get here?"

"Well, after I saw the two of you get taken by those goons in the parking lot, I followed the van. When I noticed they were heading towards the estate, I remembered I had Maria's number on that list of contact numbers you gave me before you left for England. I called her and told her what had happened, and she and her husband, Alberto here..." Pete said, now throwing his arm around the stranger jubilantly, "...Snuck me into the house and told me to wait in the dining room until the drug kicked in."

Maria's husband Alberto was almost identical to his wife in height and build. A thick mat of jet-black hair sat atop a kind and humble face that due to his profession had been weather-beaten by the sun. Helen had always said he and Maria were saints, and although he could speak very little English, it was obvious from his gentle demeanor he was a good and honest man.

"Well, thank you, Alberto..." James said shaking his hand, "...thank you all. Things were going badly, I was beginning to run out of options... by the way, what did you mean, Pete, when you said, 'wait until the drug kicked in?'"

Maria answered excitedly, clasping her hands together as she spoke, "I drugged all of them with de coffee. I no put any in your cups."

"What did you give them?" Helen asked, sheer relief making

her chuckle, although she was still shaking.

"Is a juice from the Hacaranda cactus, I get it from Mexico. I no sleep good at night. It taste like water. One drop in some 'ot milk at night will make you sleep like a baby… I give all of them ten drops each. They sleep a very, very, very long time!"

The longer James stood over the anesthetized Erik, the more relief transformed into a strong desire for retribution. It was hard to imagine as he lay there slumbering peacefully, he could have been directly responsible for so much pain and suffering. An image of Paul, Sheryl and Scott came into his mind, and an avalanche of anger consumed him. Sensing the escalating animosity emanating from him, Helen broke off her conversation with Maria and hurried over to him and asked casually, "So, what's the plan, James?"

Snapping out of his trance, he blinked several times as though he had been hypnotized, and collected his thoughts. "The article will be electronically mailed in less than five hours, and once that's out in the open, hopefully all of this will be investigated. In the meantime, I think our best course of action would be to get across the border to Mexico, and bide our time until we're sure the tide has turned in our favor."

"That seems to be what everybody else is thinking too… When Maria got the call from Pete, she told him to park your car at the south wall's service gate and wait for Alberto."

"Good… Okay, so it's still there then."

"Yes. She also told him to pack up their SUV and park it at the rear of the house. They're going to go back to Mexico for good - their sons and grandchildren are all there, she said the only reason she stayed was because of me."

"Well, then that's settled… Our only problem now, is going to be the border patrol. Erik will have alerted everyone and they're sure to be on the lookout for us."

"Pete said the same thing, and so Maria and Alberto are going to pick up a friend who knows a drivable route through the mountains. They said for us to meet them at Jacumba, which is about eighty miles east of here."

"Sounds like a good plan. Is Pete coming with us?"

"Yes, he's found the keys to a four-wheel drive SUV, so he's going to bring that – just in case the terrain is too difficult for the cars."

Walking briskly out of the room, Pete said, "C'mon everybody, we'd better get going... that weirdo's out there somewhere and I don't think he's going to give up that easily."

Before leaving James picked up Karl's brief case, removed the CD he retrieved from Arthur, and shoved it into his pocket. Pausing for a moment he noticed the large collection of files and folders within, then, slamming it shut he tucked it under his arm and hurried after them.

***

After stumbling out into the inky darkness, Karl headed directly towards the nearest lights that glowed dimly through the windows of Maria and Alberto's cottage. The door was not locked and hurtling in he made straight for the telephone and called the Ranch for reinforcements. From this location he had a clear view through the window of the front of the main house, and as he watched, he paced the room agitatedly, clenching his fists, his teeth grinding so tightly the muscles in his jaw constantly flinched. The fine line between sanity and insanity had been crossed, and it was hard to say at this stage whether he bore more malice towards his adversaries or Erik. Either way, he now knew exactly what he had to do – exterminate, without exception, all possible threats.

Seeing Maria and Alberto's car travel down the drive and out through the main gate left him feeling confused and suspicious, so he waited impatiently to see what would happen next. He didn't have to wait long – after a few minutes, Pete came out with his gun raised, and looking around cautiously, made his way to the row of vehicles parked in front of the manor and systematically slashed the tires of all but the one he was commandeering. Then, getting in and starting the engine, he beckoned to James and Helen who dashed out, climbed in the back, and they pulled away.

Furious, Karl bolted out of the cottage, and ran across the broad lawn, towards the front gate hoping to cut them off. He knew it was a futile attempt, but charged on heedlessly, the frantic thudding of his footsteps muffled by the springy turf. Then, suddenly he tripped and fell – landing heavily on a large rosebush. The spiky thorns snagged his clothes and dug viciously into his flesh. With a savage cry of pain and frustration he watched the vehicle sweep through the gates and head off down the dark lane. Tearing himself free, he turned and sprinted back towards the cottage where he noticed Alberto's white landscaping van. Panting laboriously, he clambered in, found the keys in the ignition, where they were always left, and with a screeching of tires headed out of the estate and off in the direction of the rapidly disappearing taillights.

Chapter 44

Glancing over his shoulder, Pete pulled the black sport-utility up alongside James' car. James and Helen jumped out and climbed into the car, and in less than a minute they pulled away, with Pete in the lead. Parked a few cars back, Karl watched the transfer, and as they moved away, he slowly pulled the old landscaping van into the stream of traffic. Cold hard logic seemed to have returned temporarily to win out over blind fury, and he remained several cars behind as they traveled through the brightly lit streets of La Jolla. He knew if he made his move now, he could incur unwanted police interference – and annihilation rather than apprehension was now his modus operandi.

He continued to trail along behind them at a discreet distance, far back until at last they were over the mountains and on an open and desolate stretch of freeway cutting through the desert. Then, after checking there was no sign of any other headlights in either direction, he sped up and without warning rammed James' car hard from behind. The car jarred forward and swerved to the right under the force of the impact shaking James and Helen badly. Looking round, her eyes wide with fear, Helen saw the white van approaching again. "James, it's him, what are we going to do?" she shouted desperately.

"Hang on, Helen," he replied, glancing into the rearview mirror and speeding up. He flattened his foot on the accelerator and although he initially made some headway, the landscaping van had a large eight-cylinder engine and the distance between them soon began to narrow. Closing in on them again Karl leaned out of the driver's window, stretched his arm at full length, and took a few wild shots at the rear of James' car. Fortunately, he was still not close enough and the bullets ricocheted harmlessly off the back.

Pete, who had seen what was happening slowed down to allow James to pass and then quickly maneuvered his vehicle so it was now between the two of them. The three cars flew down the empty freeway at speeds now in excess of a hundred miles per hour. Using his rearview mirror, Pete waited until Karl was directly behind him, and then violently slammed his foot down hard on the brakes. Any normal driver would have applied their breaks with full force and swerved to avoid a crash but Karl, his madness now spurring him on, maintained his speed, aligning the van so that the impact was straight on.

It was difficult to say which vehicle came off better from the collision. The old van Karl was driving was badly dented but had a lot more steel in its frame, whereas Pete's sport-utility, although a lot newer, had lost an entire wing and its rear end was now concave. Also, the additional safety features – primarily designed to protect the occupants – now proved to be a burden as Pete struggled with the deployed airbags, at the same time desperately trying to bring the vehicle back under control.

Frantically trying to steer with one hand, he reached into his pocket and pulled out his penknife, then flicking it open, plunged it deeply into the airbag, hearing a loud hissing noise as it deflated. Glancing back over his shoulder he could see Karl right on his tail, his remaining rear running lights illuminating the maniacal expression on his face as he prepared to slam into him again. Not confident his SUV would survive another violent encounter, he decided to adopt a different strategy. So, he removed his gun, lowered the passenger window and began to pump the accelerator hoping to convince his pursuer he was now having engine trouble.

It worked! Taking the bait, Karl swerved past him, accelerated, and steered a direct path to James' car. This was the opportunity Pete had been waiting for, and as Karl passed Pete, he turned and fired off every shot in his handgun. The rounds shattered the windows in Karl's van, and one shot ripped into Karl's shoulder. The impact of the bullet threw him off the steering wheel and the van veered off and careened into a concrete side barricade. Fortunately for him, the van was strong enough to realign and keep it on course long enough for him to sit back up, retake the wheel and carry on, his shattered and bloodied arm now hanging limply at his side.

Karl's eyes narrowed as he looked up at the rear-view mirror and saw Pete speeding towards him. He was proving to be a nuisance that would need to be dealt with first if he wanted to get to James and Helen. Smiling grimly to himself, he allowed Pete to catch up with him, and when he was within about twenty feet, lifted his knees to hold the steering wheel in place, turned, and shot twice at the lock holding the double doors closed at the back of the van.

When the doors swung open, Karl pumped the accelerator several times to dislodge the contents. A lawnmower, weed-eater, blower, and a variety of other gardening implements rolled out, landing directly in Pete's path. At this high speed, he had no choice but to run straight over them, and this forced the right side of the vehicle to bounce up violently as the wheels rode over the obstacles. When the front end came back in contact with the asphalt, a violent thud could be heard, the strain of which blew out a front tire flipping the vehicle over and onto its side. The metal frame grinding against the pavement made an unearthly screeching sound and generated a fountain of sparks that lit up the freeway like fireworks.

For a split-second Karl seemed indecisive, but then brought his van abruptly to a stop, watching in frustration as James' car disappeared into the distance. Steering with his only useful arm, he reversed to the mangled and twisted remains of Pete's vehicle and aligned his headlights so they lit up the overturned cab.

James, who had heard the crash and seen the subsequent sparks, had also stopped and was now reversing back at full speed towards Pete's position. Their braking distance at that high speed however, had put them quite far ahead, and as they raced backwards the image through the rear window slowly expanded. Karl dragged himself from his van, his jacket sleeve now dripping blood, walked to the wreckage and came face-to-face with Pete, who was injured but attempting to remove himself. Still speeding backwards, James and Helen stared helplessly and both shouted, "NO!" as Karl lifted his gun and cold-bloodedly fired several shots into Pete, who made a vain attempt to protect himself with his hands, before his body slumped.

Chapter 45

Frozen in shock at witnessing the heartless slaying of Pete, James stared in stunned silence through the rear window of his car at the wreckage, while Helen sobbed hysterically. They had stopped about a hundred yards from Karl, who on seeing their return, spun around violently and rushed towards them, eager to take advantage of their apparent immobility. His inert arm impeded his agility but not his ability, and without a moment's hesitation he began firing. One of the projectiles pierced the rear window and shattered the glass, spurring James into action. Shouting to Helen to duck, he slammed his foot down on the accelerator, but instead of this action propelling them away from their assailant it sent them shooting backwards at full speed towards him. This accidental blunder caught everyone off guard, throwing James and Helen violently forward in their seats, and forcing Karl to make a haphazard dive headlong into a side ditch.

He landed heavily on his wounded arm, sending a searing pain through his body and incapacitating him long enough for James to slip the gear shift into drive, and speed off. Looking back, Helen could see Karl scrambling out of the ditch and dashing towards the van. "Oh God, James, what are we going to do? He'll kill us too!" she sobbed, her voice trembling uncontrollably.

"I know."

"Are we very far from where Maria and Alberto said they'd meet us?"

233

"Let me check," he answered turning on the car's navigation system, feeding in the destination, and then studying the route and time-to-arrival. "We're still thirty-three miles away, which at this speed should take us about twenty minutes."

"Well, what can we do James? He's getting closer," she said looking back at the set of headlights that were getting noticeably brighter with each passing moment.

Staring ahead and frowning thoughtfully, he gripped the steering wheel so tightly his knuckles gleamed white. When he eventually answered, the words were muttered indistinctly, and appeared to be directed towards himself. "I'm going ninety-five now, and he's still gaining on me... the problem is, he's got nothing to lose. He drives not caring whether he lives or dies – and that gives him the advantage. Going faster would be too dangerous at this time of night, and any error on my part will be... Damn, come on, think, THINK!" His eyes flicked back and forth between the view ahead, the rear-view mirror, and the miniature car on his navigation display. "I wonder? Yes, yes, it should work."

"What James? For God's sake tell me what you're thinking!" Her voice sounded shrill.

"Look at this," he said pointing to the display that showed a small break in one of the lines on the top of the map. "There's an intersection coming up. You see this path here – if I take this road on the left, it will pass directly over the freeway."

"But it shows a construction symbol on the other side."

"If I get more information, let's see what it says... You see – perfect."

"I don't understand."

"We need an edge, and this system will give it to us. We know a section of the bridge is missing but he doesn't, and... ah, here it comes now – hold on."

A barricade and several flashing lights blocked the exit on the left of the freeway. Purposely smashing through the only sign that warned of the danger, James cruised up the slope and onto the overpass. Karl now had their car in sight, and was recklessly increasing his speed to close the gap between them. The moment James had cleared the top of the overpass and was out of Karl's sight, he pushed hard on his brakes, anxiously searching the road ahead as the car's momentum carried them forward. The headlights gradually brought the missing section of the bridge into view, and he and Helen glanced at each other in panic.

"We're not going to make it… unless!" he yelled pulling the steering wheel hard to the right, forcing the car into a sideways skid to arrest its momentum. After screeching to a stop, James turned his head slowly to the left breathing heavily as he examined with relief the ten feet of concrete still remaining between them and the edge. "Quickly, lights off, and let's get out of the way!" he shouted turning off his headlights, and pulling the car forward behind some construction equipment, parked off to the side.

Twisting their heads sharply, they looked up at the peak of the overpass and waited in silence. For a time it seemed as though he was never going to appear, but then, in the distance a dull glow of headlights appeared, followed by a small engine drone that at first was hardly discernible, but then began to rise exponentially. Holding hands tightly they waited breathlessly, their attention drawn quickly to the crest as the roar of an engine and the glare of headlights came hurtling in their direction.

Not seeing James' taillights ahead, Karl pressed harder on the already floored accelerator, his speed assisted by the now downhill run. When he finally glimpsed the approaching chasm, he immediately slammed on his brakes – but it was too late. James and Helen heard a loud squeal of the locked tires, and saw the resulting gray plume rise, almost completely obscuring their view of the van. It was at that moment Karl caught sight of them out of the corner of his eye, and quickly assessing the futility of his predicament, made one last desperate bid, motivated by duty and dementia. Choosing to no longer control the vehicle, he lifted his Luger and fired frenziedly through the broken side window as many times as he could, before the white van plummeted through the breach, tumbling into the darkness, and slamming into the bank below.

Chapter 46

The suspension squeaked and the car rocked and rolled as James drove off the road and headed slowly down the shallow ravine towards the twisted and tangled debris that lay strewn across the desert floor. Engine oil and gasoline had ignited and splattered in all directions setting up what looked like hundreds of small campfires. A cloud of dust and smoke hung over the van's metal frame, which had been severely contorted by the force of the impact and now bore no resemblance to its original form.

The faint but easily distinguishable odor of burning petroleum began to seep through the cars ventilation system, stimulating their olfactory organs and signaling an air of danger. "James, let's not… let's just go," Helen blurted out, grabbing his arm tightly.

Stopping the car, he shrugged away defiantly, "No… I want to know he's dead. I'm not going to be looking over my shoulder for the rest of my life… just stay here, Helen."

The density of the fumes issuing from the burning materials was almost asphyxiating at some points, so James lifted his jacket over his nose and mouth to filter out the unwanted toxins. Weaving his way around the obstacles, he cautiously approached from the rear, and found Karl semi-conscious, still sitting upright in the driver's seat of the van, his chest heaving erratically. On first glance his injuries appeared to be minor, but on closer inspection James could see four metal spikes protruding from his chest, the result of being impaled from behind by a garden fork.

Just as James was about to turn and leave, he noticed a small black book hanging out of Karl's ripped inside jacket pocket. Unable to reach it from outside, he climbed into the cab through an opening and drew closer. Now face to face with Karl, he could see blood trickling from his nose and mouth. Air bubbles were rising through the blood from his chest wounds, and he could hear him fighting the fluid in his lungs in his battle for breath.

As James leaned forward and reached for the book, Karl seemed to suddenly become aware of his presence – his eyes sprang wide open and he grabbed James tightly around the neck, thrusting his thumbs forcefully against his Adam's apple. Unable to break the strength of his death grip, James lifted his feet to Karl's chest and pushed with all his might. The hold was released almost instantly, and Karl froze in excruciating pain as the fork was driven further into his body.

Surprisingly still conscious but wheezing horribly, he fixed a malevolent stare on James, and straining for oxygen mumbled, "Eh Ah… Eh Ah… Eh, you can't win, Ah. Eh, We're too powerful, ah…"

Deciding this last pathetic brag did not deserve a response, James took the book from his jacket, placed it in his pocket and climbed out of the wreck through a side aperture.

"Eh, You lost your friends, Ah," Karl said, striving for a weak smile. "Eh, I can still see him begging for his life… Ah… just before I killed him, Ah… Eh, Pete, wasn't it? … Ah." Grimacing in agony as a bout of coughing wracked his body he continued to provoke, blood spitting from his mouth, "Eh… And your other friends, Barnes… Ah… Eh… his wife was Jewish… Ah… Eh… A fitting end don't you think – just like the good old days… Ah."

Paralyzed by the sheer force of disbelief at what he had just heard, James turned back, feeling an uncontrollable rage build and swell within him. For the first time in his life, he had an overwhelming urge to kill, and noticing Karl's gun at the side of him, he reached down and picked it up. Pushed beyond control, he leveled the gun and aimed it directly at Karl's head. He was about to fire with no compunction, when Helen shouted, "James – don't do it!"

With very little constraint left he yelled vehemently, "He HAS to die, Helen."

"Put the gun down, James," she said calmly, walking towards him.

"NO – somebody has to do something about this evil bastard... He started killing when he was a teenager and he's never stopped. He's destroyed too many lives... Damn, when I think of what he did to Paul, Sheryl and Scott, and now Pete."

"You can't, James."

"But don't you see Helen – that's why his type win. You and I don't think like they do. They have no conscience restraining their actions, no compassion for anyone – they go through life not abiding by any rules of human decency. Well... justice is finally going to catch up with this maniac."

"This makes you no better than him."

"If that's what it takes... then so be it."

"Okay... as long as you can step over to the other side, and still find your way back... because I don't think there is a way back... and anyway, look at him, he's dying – he'll be dead in a few minutes."

James' grip on the gun got tighter and tighter, until his hand began to shake, and then in a burst of frustration and anger he threw the gun down and turned away. Stumbling over the rough rock-strewn land, Helen approached him and took his arm.

"Come on, James… let's go." Pulling him back towards the car they both took a final look at Karl who was now muttering something incoherently in German.

Stopping in his tracks, James smacked his hand against his head, "Wait a minute… we're missing an opportunity here." Running back to his car, he grabbed the mind-link suitcase from the back seat.

"No… please, what are you doing, James?" Helen asked as he began setting up the system next to Karl.

"You gave me the idea, Helen – you said he was dying. They say your whole life is meant to flash before you at this time. Well, let's see what's going through his mind at this moment. Hopefully, I can get some more information."

Karl had now slipped into unconsciousness, his eyes flickered and there was no resistance as James leaned into the cab and positioned the primary headset on him. Crouching down, he placed the repeating headset on himself, turned on the system, and waited.

The familiar sensation began, but this time more violently, and the Mind Link images spiraled down uncontrollably, with twisted pictures spun into tornado like funnels randomly leaping forward and attempting to lock into place, accompanied by a deafening onslaught of slurred voices and sounds. Random visions in no chronological order stabilized for a short time showing violent acts intermixed with ordinary activities. The exchange rate slowly increased, not giving James much time to decipher their location, time index or connection. Many people, not known, seen over and over, such as an irritable and disapproving woman.

And then a very familiar image appeared – that of the cliffs in Cornwall and Helga on the cliffs watching Colin's fishing boat on the horizon. The blustery wind masked the approach of Karl who grabbed her by the arm. As she turned and recognized him a look of horror crossed her face. In vain, she attempted to get away from her stronger captor, who seemed to be toying with her – trapped perilously on the cliffs edge. In an unexpected reversal, and with renewed vigor, she accepted her fate, grabbed her attacker by the lapels and tried to take him with her over the edge. They struggled for a moment, and he almost lost his footing, but he soon won out, held her out at arm's length over the side, her toes struggling for a foothold, before letting her go to plummet to her death.

The image now cut to a high mountain retreat, looking out to the Andes. Older men and woman group together for a photograph. The older Karl was among them, and then Erik, a few years younger appeared to hand over a shield showing FAHNENBRUEDER emblazoned across the shield.

Another rapid switch and three thousand pupils were attending a school assembly at Ordensburg. Standing center stage, flanked by the faculty, a senior-ranking Gestapo officer listens proudly as the pupils sing their rousing school anthem, which was accompanied by rhythmic stomps that were almost deafening. At its conclusion, the officer began his address, praising a young man for completing a successful front line loan assignment, and then a fourteen-year-old Kurt Dietl was called to the stage and presented with a medal, to the drowning applause of the school body.

The Mind Link blacked out, and James was about to remove it when a new scene showed Pete's father, a commanding older man with the look of a retired policeman, looking weary as he entered his downtown office late in the evening. Turning on the desk lamp he sat down and began working on a report and looked up as the door creaked open. Seeing only the muzzle of a gun he lunged for a drawer but was repelled by an accurate shot that whips back his reaching arm. As he attempted to reach across, now a lot more sluggishly with his other arm, a shot was fired directly into his stomach.

Pete's father's body shook uncontrollably but his face was resolute and he stared down the assailant who moved around the desk and kicked the wheeled office chair so it slammed up against the wall. Karl pressed the gun's muzzle into a carefully chosen position in his chest – directly above his heart.

Still conscious, Pete's father looked down at the vintage Luger handgun, up at the gunman with hooded eyes of defiance, and spat in his face.

"Bravo, you die well," was heard before the crack and thud of the fatal shot.

The image sped back in time and the sound of bombs raining down high above overwhelm the next sequence, in which Karl seemed to be receiving instructions from several high ranking German officers. In front of them, was a large map of Argentina and the word FAHNENBRUEDER on a table and some papers, which had a distinctive logo blending the letters U S A into the swastika.

New scenes were now substituted with others at a rapidly increasing rate, and then the erratic cyclone seemed to suddenly buckle and empty into an abyss, leaving behind it blankness. Removing the headset, he turned to Karl, whose breathing had stopped – he was dead.

Helen was staring at James looking shocked and disturbed "He stopped breathing a few minutes ago… I don't want to stay in Mexico any longer than we have to… I want to get back as soon as possible and set the record straight."

Reaching out his hand, "I know, love, I know, hopefully it won't be for too long."

Chapter 47

Two Months Later…

A heavy early morning mist had settled over Southampton pier, transforming the moored ships and buildings into phantoms. Although it was the middle of June, a bitter wind cut into James and Helen, forcing them to huddle into their jackets and cram their hands deep into their pockets.

They waited on the deck, eager now to disembark. It had been a long cruise and although the cargo ship did not have the amenities of a luxury liner, it did have a quality that was far more important to them at this time – anonymity. Leaning on the rail and gazing out across the endless rows of warehouses, James laughed quietly. Reclining against the rail, Helen brushed a strand of hair out of her eyes, and looked at him questioningly.

"What were you thinking about?"

"I was just remembering something Paul told me years ago."

"What was that?"

"Nothing of any importance, it was just a story he used in his lectures to describe "negative logic". I don't even know what made me think of it."

"Tell me."

"Well, it happened years ago when Scott was about five. They had returned from a trip to the mountains, and had stopped off to get some cakes at The Alpine Bakery. When they got home, Sheryl had apparently taken her cake, and just as Paul went to get his, Scott rushed over and snatched away the larger one of the two. Trying to teach his son a lesson in etiquette, Paul said, 'that wasn't very nice of you Scott. Now if I had got there first, I would have taken the smaller cake.' Confused with his dad's reasoning, Scott apparently replied in all innocence, '…but you've got the smaller cake, Dad?'"

They both chuckled, and for a split second his friends were reborn through a memory. Their happiness however, was short-lived, and as their laughter died away and reality reestablished itself, James' face dropped and his countenance changed to reveal a deep sadness. "Paul, Sheryl, Scott, and Pete…" he spoke softly, his voice breaking slightly, "…I don't want to forget them, but I can't bear thinking about them."

"I know, James," she said, her face drawn and pensive.

"So… should we let it be and move on?"

"I'd say there's a very good chance that Erik won't!"

"I think you're probably right… maybe we shouldn't either."

Turning away, she paused, reluctant to bring up the inescapable truth that now plagued her night and day. "And… what about the fact that… I mean, you know who I am now, James."

"As far as I'm concerned Helen, you're just you – a completely different person to your father, and your grandfather for that matter. In fact, you couldn't be more opposite, and if you're wondering how I feel about it… I love you, because you're a warm, loving and compassionate person… all the things they are not, nor ever could be."

Noticing she looked cold, he pulled her towards him and put his arms around her. Together they looked towards the large sign that read, 'Welcome to Southampton.'

"Everything will be fine, Helen."

"I know it will… we have each other."

***

It was a warm, sunny day in Southern California, and any vestige of clouds were burnt off quickly as the day wore on. A reporter and a TV cameraman ran up to Erik Banner as he walked to his car. Lifting a hand to shield his eyes from the sun, he smiled warmly as they approached, pausing to allow a brief interview.

"Can you give us a moment, Mayor Banner?"

"Sure, guys."

"The polls show you well ahead – any comments?"

"What can I say? I'm very pleased – let's keep it that way!"

"How about your critics who say you're too tough on some issues?"

"Voters want a strong leader who isn't scared to make the tough choices."

"How would you respond to your opponent, who says you lack a moral core?"

"I think the moment somebody starts attacking you personally they haven't got a good argument."

"And what of the story printed by several newspapers and magazines, linking you to several murders and alleging you are the son of…"

Interrupting and laughing good-naturedly. "I'm not the first, and I definitely won't be the last victim of a cheap smear campaign. I read the story – it was a good work of fiction… It did wonders for my campaign – I couldn't have afforded to buy that amount of media coverage… I'll tell you something," climbing into his limousine and leaning out for the final comment, "I hope the same thing happens when I decide to run for a higher office!"

Pulling smoothly into moderate mid-day traffic, the sedan turned left on Market Street, passed Horton Plaza, and after traveling through several intersections pulled up outside a French restaurant, La Pomme D'amor. This converted Victorian Villa was set back from the street by a small lawn enclosed by a brick wall, bordered by bright spring flowers. Erik exited the car and walked up the center path, through the open entrance, and into the foyer. The lobby was cluttered with portraits, books and furniture, that combined seemed to be trying a little too hard to look French. Spying the person he had arranged to meet already seated on the veranda, he strolled across the restaurant, weaving between the crowded tables, and out through the latticed double glass doors.

"Mr. Banner."

"Good to see you."

"You too, sir."

"Your sons? Prospering I hope?"

"Doing very well, thank you for remembering them, sir."

"What did you find out?"

The view of the woman was at first obstructed by posts, plants, other guests, and finally a menu, but eventually she was revealed as… Maria. Gone was the broken English, the unkempt hair and casual attire – replaced with a look and an air of sophisticated professional exactness.

"Peter Hammond is still alive – assisted by a friend, a detective Sam Patterson. Alberto is following up on a lead he is recovering in a medical clinic in the Ensenada area."

"Find him quickly, and take care of that loose end… so you finally received a letter from her?"

"Yes, I e-mailed you a copy."

"It's been quite an inconvenience losing, Karl."

"You don't think he would have changed his position?"

"No, he would have insisted Helen be killed – I just needed her out of the way until this election is finished... I have been told a replacement has been selected – a woman, no less!"

"I'm glad to hear that, sir."

"How would you like to move to England?"

"I'd like that very much... My assignment?"

"Resuming your role, of course, as ... the guardian."